'I'd like us to enjoy each moment we spend together, without looking too far into the future. Isn't that what you would like too?'

Lucy looked up into his dark, expressive eyes. 'Yes, that's what I want.'

'So, that's what we'll have.' Vittorio bent his head and kissed her.

She savoured the touch of his lips in that brief moment. She wondered briefly how long she would be able to be part of a temporary relationship like this. One where only the present mattered. Was she making another disastrous mistake?

If she could hold on to her deep emotions, if she could prevent herself from falling in love with Vittorio, she could enjoy this light-hearted affair. Was the risk worth taking?

Dear Reader

Ah, Rome! One of my favourite cities—and one of the most romantic! The atmosphere is electric, exciting, invigorating. It's a city where couples in love like to spend long, lazy weekends walking along the fascinating streets, visiting the awesome temples and palaces, perhaps lingering beside the Trevi Fountain before returning to some cosy hotel where romance is always on the menu.

THE ITALIAN SURGEON'S SECRET is the second book in my Italian duo about twin English sisters Sarah and Lucy, both doctors, who find themselves in the same Roman hospital, set beside the Tiber river, and fall in love amidst the energy of the Accident and Emergency department.

I hope you enjoy reading these two books as much as I have enjoyed writing them.

Margaret Barker

ROMAN HOSPITAL

The romance of Rome, the excitement of A&E!

Recent titles by the same author:

DR FELLINI'S PREGNANT BRIDE
  (Book 1 of *Roman Hospital*)
THE GREEK DOCTOR'S BRIDE
THE FRENCH SURGEON'S SECRET CHILD

THE ITALIAN SURGEON'S SECRET

BY
MARGARET BARKER

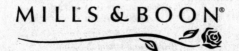

MILLS & BOON®

First published in Great Britain 2004
Harlequin Mills & Boon Limited,
Eton House, 18-24 Paradise Road, Richmond, Surrey TW9 1SR

© Margaret Barker 2004

ISBN 0 263 83922 2

Set in Times Roman 10½ on 12 pt.
03-0904-49136

Printed and bound in Spain
by Litografia Rosés, S.A., Barcelona

CHAPTER ONE

'I'VE just been to see your wonderful baby in the special care baby unit,' Lucy said, sitting down at the side of her twin sister's bed. 'Charlotte's still in her incubator but she's breathing extremely well. Incredible to believe she was eight weeks premature! I delivered a few prems when I was working in Obstetrics but never one as beautiful and perfectly formed as Charlotte.'

Sarah propped herself up on her pillows and smiled. 'Me, too, but, then, I'm biased, aren't I? Perhaps you are, Aunty Lucy. Charlotte's very tiny, but that's only to be expected. A bit wrinkly, don't you think?'

Lucy smiled. 'Oh, she's beautiful! You must be absolutely delighted with her. I'm so proud of you, Sarah, my little sister, after all you've been through.'

'Not so much of the little! I'm only ten minutes younger than you and I must weigh twice as much at the moment!'

'You look lovely, Sarah, honestly! The few pounds you put on with the baby will soon melt away.'

'Oh, I'm so glad you're here!' Lucy reached for her sister's hand and squeezed it. 'It was so good of you to give up your job and come out to cover my maternity leave.'

'Sarah, I needed a break. I needed to get away for a while and…' Lucy broke off. 'Look, you don't want to hear my problems.'

'Oh, but I do! You've never seemed to have any problems. You've always been the capable one, the positive one, the supergirl who goes successfully through life. Please, tell me why you wanted to get away.'

Lucy hesitated. She hated to appear vulnerable and she didn't want to burden Sarah with her problems.

'Let's just say I had an affair with a love rat. A man who conned me into thinking…thinking he was something he wasn't. Like an idiot, I fell for him but it's all over now.'

'Are you sure?'

'Absolutely!' Lucy said in what she hoped was a convincing voice. The technicalities of the affair were over but she was still bleeding inside.

'And one day will you tell me all the gory details?'

'One day I will.'

Lucy swallowed hard. One day when the hurt had gone away she'd have a heart-to-heart with her sister.

'But not now, Sarah, when we're here to celebrate the birth of your wonderful daughter.'

'Will you be Charlotte's godmother?'

Lucy smiled. 'There's nothing I'd like more.'

Vanessa, sister in charge of Obstetrics at the Ospedale Tevere in Rome, came into Sarah's room, smiling at the two sisters as she spoke in rapid, clipped Italian.

'I thought I was seeing double when you arrived this morning, Dottore Lucy. You are so like your sister. Long blonde hair, blue eyes, same slim figure that Sarah had when she first started working here at the hospital. Tell me, Dottore Lucy, when you went to see your baby niece, did it make you feel you would like to have your own little bambino?'

Lucy swallowed hard. So often, recently, people had made casual remarks that touched a raw nerve.

'I haven't time for babies,' Lucy said in Italian, speaking slowly, clearly and carefully so that she wouldn't make any mistakes. 'I'm a full-time working woman.'

Sister Vanessa nodded. 'Like me. I must go and do some more work. I just wanted to check that Sarah had everything she needed.'

'I'm fine! *Tutto bene!*' Sarah said.

Lucy resumed their conversation in English after Sister Vanessa had gone out of the room. 'I ought to report for duty now. Don't want to be late on my first day in...what do you call Accident and Emergency again?'

'Pronto Soccorso. Carlos is down there now.'

'Carlos delivered baby Charlotte, didn't he?'

Sarah smiled fondly. 'Yes. He was wonderful.'

'A perfect ending to a true romance!'

'More like the beginning of a new life together,' Sarah said, unable to conceal her happiness. 'We're going to be married soon and Carlos wants to adopt Charlotte. Her biological father has given his permission so we can go ahead.'

'Oh, Sarah, I'm so happy for you!' Lucy hugged her sister. 'You've been so brave, carrying on working at the hospital here throughout your pregnancy, making plans to be a single mother and bringing up Charlotte by yourself. And how clever of you to have Charlotte on our thirtieth birthday. What a fantastic birthday present!'

'Totally unplanned, as you can imagine! Couldn't believe I was in labour yesterday. I was sure it was simply backache!'

'First-time mothers!' Lucy said, giving a wry grin. 'We've met them, haven't we?'

Sarah laughed. 'It's much easier being a doctor than a patient where pregnancy and childbirth are concerned. But you know, Lucy, Carlos has been so supportive all the way through my pregnancy. And then when we found we were falling in love…well…'

She broke off, her voice choking with emotion.

'You deserve your happiness,' Lucy said. 'When we were teenagers I remember you had a crush on Carlos but you thought he was too old for you because he was nine years older than we were.'

'It was you who had to convince me that Carlos wouldn't even consider a youngster like me, Lucy.'

'Did I?' Lucy frowned as she tried to remember what she'd said all those years ago. 'I'm sorry if I put you off the idea.'

Sarah shrugged. 'All water under the bridge now. You were quite right at the time. I was too young for Carlos then. Since I came out to Rome, it's been wonderful getting to know him in a completely different way. Falling in love with him was… Sorry, Lucy, you don't want to hear me going all romantic, do you?'

Lucy smiled. 'You can be as romantic as you like. I'm so happy for you. Now, take it easy. You only gave birth yesterday so move slowly when you get up. Take a wheelchair when you go down to see Charlotte. Oh, and remember to drink plenty of fluids.'

Sarah grinned. 'Yes, Doctor. I'll behave like the perfect patient.'

Lucy kissed her sister's cheek. 'See you later.'

'Good luck!'

'Thanks. I may need it!'

As Sarah followed the signs for Pronto Soccorso, she began to feel apprehensive. She had no qualms about her ability as a doctor, but her Italian was a bit rusty. She'd been fluent when she was younger, having spent most of her summer holidays at the house her family had rented on the coast. But she hadn't used her Italian much as an adult.

The Italian classes she'd attended over the last few weeks and the Italian medical books she'd been reading had been helpful. But in the chaotic atmosphere of Accident and Emergency, when patients were arriving with alarming speed and medical colleagues were calling out for her help, how would she cope with the language?

She was soon to find out! She took a deep breath as she pushed open the swing doors and went into Pronto Soccorso.

A thin, wiry, middle-aged woman, dressed in an impeccably ironed white sister's uniform, was coming out of the office near the door. She moved quickly towards Lucy, a slightly perplexed expression on her face.

Lucy cleared her throat. '*Io sono Dottore* Lucy Montgomery.'

The sister smiled and began speaking rapidly in Italian, explaining that she had thought that Lucy was Sarah, which had confused her because she'd just heard that Sarah was in the obstetrics ward. Lucy found she could understand better than she'd imagined she would. Her confidence was restored as she listened to Sister Sabina introducing herself and explaining that Dr Carlos Fellini, the medical director of Pronto Soccorso, had asked if Lucy would go to his office as soon as she arrived.

Sister Sabina accompanied Lucy to the door of Carlos's office.

'Lucy, do come in!' Carlos said in the calm, steady, strongly accented English she remembered he'd used when she'd been a child staying in the house owned by his parents.

Carlos stood up, indicating one of the seats at the side

of his desk. Another man was occupying a chair at the other side of Carlos's desk.

'Let me introduce you to our orthopaedic consultant, Vittorio Vincenzi. Vittorio, this is Dr Lucy Montgomery.'

'You must be Sarah's twin sister,' Vittorio said in perfect but charmingly accented English. 'You are so very much alike.'

Vittorio had stood up when she'd entered the room. He now held out his hand towards her. She felt a firm grasp, cool smooth skin. As she looked up she saw handsome, striking, olive-skinned features, a chiselled determined jaw. Vittorio's mouth was slightly open, revealing strong white teeth, his lips curling up at the sides in an approximation of a smile. But the expression in his eyes was far from smiley. Lucy detected a deep sadness that was almost palpable.

Perhaps it was because she was constantly having to fight against her own sadness that she instinctively knew that Vittorio had suffered, too. And his suffering was ongoing, as hers was if she allowed herself to wallow in self-pity.

Which she never did! Well, just occasionally she allowed herself a quiet weep about the past. Especially if she was feeling particularly tired, she found herself letting down her emotional guard. Especially about the baby. The baby she'd so longed for. The baby that Mother Nature had decided wasn't strong enough to survive in this difficult world.

'Carlos tells me you are here for three months to cover Sarah's maternity leave,' Vittorio said.

'We're very fortunate that Lucy agreed to leave her English hospital and come to work at the Ospedale Tevere,' Carlos said.

Lucy moved to the other side of the desk and sat down.

'I'm looking forward to working here.'

'But your work as a senior doctor in Accident and Emergency at the hospital in England,' Vittorio persisted. 'Carlos has just been telling me about your qualifications and experience. Have you been given leave of absence from your position?'

Lucy hesitated. She hadn't even told Sarah yet but everyone would have to know sooner or later.

'Actually, I've resigned.'

Carlos raised one eyebrow. 'I had no idea, Lucy. I hope that working here hasn't disrupted your medical career.'

'Not at all! I wanted to come to Rome. I…' Again, she hesitated. 'I needed a change. To get away from…er…'

'Personal problems?' Carlos enquired.

'Exactly!'

Lucy had no idea why she was being so frank so early on in her time here at the Ospedale Tevere. Perhaps it was because she felt she was among friends and could unburden herself. Carlos was a lifelong friend who'd been so kind to Sarah and herself when they'd been small. He was soon to be her brother-in-law. And Vittorio…well, his dark, brooding, enigmatic expression was giving nothing away. Possibly her diagnosis of background suffering might have been correct.

Carlos was leaning back in his chair, his brow furrowed in thought as he watched Lucy.

'What plans have you made when Sarah's three-month maternity leave is up?'

'I haven't made any plans. I'm not thinking any further than three months ahead at the moment.'

'Good! Let's review the situation when you've been working here for a few weeks. Actually, I would prefer that Sarah took longer than three months off work so if you were available to extend your contract, that would be perfect. Sarah may not agree to taking a longer career break and, of course, I don't intend to influence her in any way, but…'

'Of course not, Carlos.' Sarah smiled. 'But I'm sure you can be very persuasive in a subtle kind of way.'

'Exactly! What I'm saying is that I would be delighted to extend your contract if Sarah agrees to stay at home with the baby for longer. So, please, don't make any further plans, Lucy, for the moment. I'll let you know when I've put forward my ideas to Sarah.'

'So you would prefer I don't discuss it with Sarah until…'

'You've understood me perfectly!' Carlos smiled, turning his head to look at Vittorio. In deference to Lucy he continued speaking in English.

'And now the question we were discussing when Lucy arrived. If you would agree to take charge of Pronto Soccorso when I'm with Sarah and baby Charlotte, I would be extremely relieved. The hospital board was very impressed with the way you took charge when I was away at the conference in Milano.'

Carlos smiled as he leaned forward. 'When I was in Milano I met several of your colleagues from the Pronto Soccorso department where you were medical director. They all spoke very highly about your time there. In particular, several doctors wished me to convey their regards and—'

'Yes, that was a very happy time for me,' Vittorio said quickly. 'Pronto Soccorso was my first career choice but…' He hesitated. 'Circumstances dictated that I change course and pursue a career in orthopaedics.'

Carlos nodded. 'I understand why you would want to do that,' he said gravely.

Lucy looked from one to the other. Neither of them was going to elaborate.

Vittorio stood up and walked over to the window, his back towards them. 'I have to admit I do enjoy working in Pronto Soccorso, but I don't want my orthopaedic patients to be neglected. I have an excellent senior doctor who could take charge of the orthopaedic department when I'm not there.'

Carlos leaned forward. 'And we'll make sure that you're available for consultation and orthopaedic surgery at any time you feel your expertise is required, Vittorio. So, what do you say?'

Vittorio swung round, striding back across the room, his hand held out towards Carlos. 'Yes, I agree.'

'*Magnifico!*'

The two men stood up and shook hands.

'So, perhaps you would take over today, Vittorio? I only got back from the conference yesterday. You've been in charge for two weeks so you are more in the picture than I am. I want to spend some time with Sarah, make arrangements for where we are going to live and— Oh!'

Carlos raised his hands in the air. '*Mamma mia!* I have so many distractions at the moment!'

Vittorio patted the side of Carlos's shoulder. '*Non si preoccupi!* Don't worry Carlos. Go and see your beautiful bride-to-be and your little treasure of a daughter. I will take charge as from now.'

Vittorio looked imperiously towards Lucy. 'Come with me, Dottore Lucy.'

Lucy stood up quickly. Here was a man who was used to taking charge. A man who wanted to get on with things. Possibly he was impatient, intolerant even? She would find out.

'*Dottore Lucy! Pronto!*' Sister Sabina called as Lucy arrived in Pronto Soccorso.

Lucy moved through the centre of the department towards the cubicle where Sister Sabina was waiting. A young child had just arrived on a trolley. The little girl was whimpering, her knees held tightly up to her chin. After hearing a brief résumé of the problems the child was suffering from, Lucy bent over her patient.

'*Dove le fa male?*' she asked gently. 'Where does it hurt, Roberta?'

'*Mi fa male lo stomaco,*' little Roberta replied.

Sister Sabina was called away at this point. Lucy glanced at the temperature reading. Too high. She palpated the child's abdomen, moving gently over to the area she suspected from the recent medical history might be the problem. Sure enough, as her fingers touched the sensitive lower right section of the abdomen between the thigh and the groin the child winced and called out.

'*No, no, no! Per favore, no!*'

'*Mi dispiace*, Roberta, I'm sorry,' Lucy said as she made a quick note that it was the right iliac fossa which was the problem area.

As she considered the other symptoms of high temperature, recent vomiting and excessive abdominal pain, she made a provisional diagnosis of appendicitis.

'Has your daughter recently had any food or drink?' Lucy asked the mother, who was leaning over the examination couch from the other side.

The mother shook her head. 'No food since yesterday and she vomited that back. Is it dangerous, Doctor?'

Lucy spoke slowly and calmly in Italian, making sure she didn't upset the mother any more than she already was.

'Roberta will be taken to the operating theatre shortly. There is a possibility that she is suffering from appendicitis.'

The mother leaned forward and clutched Lucy's hand. 'Please, take great care of my little girl, Doctor.'

'Of course we will,' Lucy said gently.

Sister Sabina had returned. Lucy spoke to her quickly and was assured that Roberta would be taken to Theatre as quickly as possible.

'Would you examine the head injury in the next cubicle, Lucy?' Sabina asked quietly. 'I'll organise the operating theatre and prepare Roberta for surgery.'

Lucy touched the side of Roberta's cheek. 'You'll soon be well again. The doctors are going to take away the pain from your stomach.'

Roberta reached out her tiny hand and clutched at Lucy's. '*Grazie, Dottore*,' she whispered, before putting her hands protectively back over her abdomen.

Lucy moved quickly into the next cubicle. It was mid-morning now. The patients were being admitted at a rapid rate, but she was used to this intense atmosphere. Her medical colleagues were doing their jobs calmly and expertly. She was no longer apprehensive. She felt she could once again cope with any emergency. Being in Italy didn't make any difference. It was all the same when you were a trained and experienced doctor.

Her next patient was a young man called Alfredo Fontana. He was lying on the examination couch and appeared totally unconscious. Lucy learned from his dis-

traught wife that he'd fallen from the first-floor balcony
of their apartment while mending the stone parapet surrounding it. She'd heard him call out and had found him
lying on the pavement below. He hadn't regained consciousness.

Lucy peeled back Alfredo's eyelids and shone a light
into his pupils. The pupils were dilated but there was no
reaction to the light. She checked his pulse and found it
to be slow and feeble. It was imperative to rehydrate her
patient as soon as possible. She put a line into his arm
and began a continuous intravenous infusion of dextrose
before rechecking his endotracheal tube. There was a
clear airway to his lungs. His blood pressure was beginning to rise but the pulse remained too slow, which in-
dicated intracranial pressure.

Lucy quickly organised an X-ray of his skull which
revealed, as she'd suspected, a fracture at the base of the
skull. The haematoma that was building up would have
to be released as soon as possible. She alerted Theatre
and requested an immediate operation.

Calmly, she explained to Alfredo's wife that surgery
would be necessary to relieve the pressure on the brain.
The young woman was now accepting the fact that everything possible was being done to save her husband.

Leaving a nurse to prepare her patient for Theatre,
Lucy moved on to her next patient. Cecilia, a woman of
thirty-five, had sustained three fractured ribs in a car
accident. Lucy examined the X-rays before beginning to
strap up Cecilia's chest. As she was doing this, she noticed a slight discharge from her patient's right nipple.

After checking that Cecilia wasn't breast-feeding or
pregnant, Lucy sent a specimen of the discharge to the
laboratory. If her suspicions were correct, this patient
might be suffering from breast cancer. She couldn't de-

tect a lump but the lesion might be too deep-seated to be detected at present. The discharge was the only possibly carcinogenic symptom so far.

It would take a couple of days for the lab to analyse all the tests she'd set up. So as not to worry her patient Lucy merely explained that it would be necessary for her to stay in the hospital to rest her ribs. If the tests proved negative the patient needn't know about the cancer scare. If the tests proved positive, Lucy would have to refer her to the hospital oncology department.

The Pronto Soccorso department had a series of small primary care units leading directly off the main area, where patients were cared for until they were either discharged or admitted to the appropriate ward. Lucy approved of the system because it meant she would be able to keep a check on Cecilia's progress and liaise with the other medical staff who were caring for her.

After making sure that her patient was settled comfortably in the primary orthopaedic unit, she hurried back to the assessment area of Pronto Soccorso. Glancing at the clock, she saw that she should have gone off duty an hour ago.

'How was your day, Lucy?'

Lucy turned round at the sound of Vittorio's voice. Her colleague was the only one on the staff who spoke such excellent English. She'd been speaking Italian constantly for most of the day. There had been a couple of English tourists who'd been very happy to find an English-speaking doctor but apart from that it had been non-stop Italian.

'It was interesting. Interesting and exhausting.'

'So you wouldn't say no to a cold glass of Frascati?'

Lucy wasn't quite sure how to take this. Whenever she'd seen Vittorio during the day he'd been decidedly professional and coldly clinical with her. Yet here he was inviting her to have a drink with him. Perhaps he felt it his duty to a foreigner in his country to thaw out a little.

'Don't tempt me. I have a few things to do before I go off duty.'

'Oh, no, you don't!'

Vittorio leaned forward and touched the lapel of her white coat. 'Remove this garment at once, Doctor. I'm in charge here and I need some company down by the river.'

She hesitated. 'Well, I would certainly like to speak English for at least an hour so I'll agree to come with you, Vittorio.'

As she pulled off her white coat, she asked Vittorio where he'd learned to speak such good English.

A veiled expression came over his eyes. 'Oh, it's a long story. I'll tell you over a drink. We'll walk along the path by the river to a little wine bar that Carlos introduced me to when I first came to the hospital. Enotecca Giovanni. I think you'll like it.'

Lucy glanced down at the cotton dress she'd been wearing since early that morning. 'I ought to go and change first. I feel pretty grubby.'

Vittorio looked perplexed. 'Grubby? What is grubby? You look pretty, yes, but I don't know…'

'It means sort of dishevelled, how you feel when you've worn the same clothes all day.'

'Oh, you look fine, Lucy! Changing clothes takes too long and I'm a very impatient man. Stay just as you are. The only change I shall make to myself is to carry the jacket of my suit as soon as we're out of here.'

Lucy glanced at his well-cut suit. It was a smooth grey, lightweight, typical Italian, hand-finished summer garment for the distinguished consultant. For a moment she almost felt as she used to do when she was setting out with a handsome personable man for the first time. A sense of excitement, wondering if at the end of the evening she would be hoping they would meet again.

But the moment passed as reality set in. It had been a long time since she'd sustained feelings like that. Mark had put paid to that! Romantic feelings happened in the books she read and the films she saw but not to her any more. It would be a long time before she would dare to go down that road again—if ever! Far too dangerous! She enjoyed the company of men, but she intended to keep herself emotionally independent.

Still, she wished she was wearing something a little more chic to complement this gorgeous Italian man. But as she left the hospital she found she was simply glad to escape into the evening sunshine after being confined inside all day.

As she fell into step beside Vittorio she glanced across to the far bank of the Tiber. The sun was glinting on the cars as they sped along the bank of the river. The noise of their horns and the occasional squeal of the brakes lingered in the evening air.

'You know, Vittorio, we could only be in one city in the world. Rome is very noisy but that's one of the things I enjoy about it. It's so…so vibrant, so lively. I love it.'

Vittorio glanced down at her. 'I prefer Milano. But that's because I was born there.'

'What made you come to Rome?'

'I… Well, like you, I needed a change…too many memories… Ah, here we are. This is Enotecca Giovanni.'

Vittorio put his hand on the small of her back and

guided her towards the entrance. For a moment Lucy enjoyed the feel of his hand against the thin cotton of her dress. It was so long since she'd felt a spontaneous frisson at the touch of a man's hand. She could almost think she was coming alive again! Maybe she should stop fighting it and go with the flow for a couple of hours. After all, this was the sort of head-turning man whom most single girls would love to spend the evening with.

A small rotund man greeted them at the door, speaking quickly in effusive Italian. Vittorio said he would like to sit out on the terrace. Giovanni brought them a bottle of Frascati and a couple of glasses, making it quite clear that the wine was on the house.

'You must be a good customer here, Vittorio,' Lucy said, sipping the deliciously cold wine.

A wistfully sad smile flitted across Vittorio's face. 'I like to escape here at the end of the day whenever I can. I watch the river, the boats, the setting sun…and I try to make my mind a complete blank.'

Lucy heard the pathos in his voice. Imbued with the courage of having drunk half a glass of the delicious wine, she leaned forward. 'Are you trying to forget the memories of your life in Milano?'

Vittorio looked startled. 'No. I never want to forget Milano. I was born there. My mother and my sisters and brothers still live there. Some of the happiest times of my life were spent there. I simply…I simply don't want to think about my life in Milano any more. I need to move on and yet…'

He picked up the bottle and topped up Lucy's glass before filling his own again.

Lucy noticed that he'd mentioned his mother, sisters and brothers. Something was missing. From the tone of his voice she instinctively knew there had been a tragedy of some kind. There had been no mention of a wife, an ex-wife, a girlfriend. And Vittorio looked as if he was bleeding inside emotionally.

She stretched out her arm across the table and covered Vittorio's hand with her own.

'Would it help to talk about it?'

Vittorio glanced down at Lucy's small, slender, smooth-skinned hand. His first instinct was to pull his own hand away. He didn't want anybody's pity. He was done with pity. It had only made him feel worse when friends and relatives had commiserated with him on his grief. And he didn't want to be roused by physical contact with another woman either.

So many women had tried to comfort him. He knew he'd always been a virile man, a man with strong sexual desires, and when a woman came on strong with him it was difficult to resist. But he knew he could never love again.

There was something about Lucy, however, that made him feel safe. She appeared calm, understanding, extremely capable. He'd watched her working today with the patients. He'd seen her listening to harrowing case histories, nodding in the right places, offering advice and comfort. She'd never forced herself on anybody or lost her patience.

Maybe she was just the sort of listening ear he needed this evening. He surprised himself by raising Lucy's hand to his lips and gently pressing them against the cool, comforting, soft skin of her palm. He looked across the table into the sensitive blue eyes and knew she wasn't the kind of woman who was trying to rouse and confuse him physically.

Lucy was beautiful, attractive, everything a man could

wish for in a woman. But that was precisely why he didn't want any complications this evening.

'I think it would help to talk,' he said, his voice husky as he felt his emotions churning around inside him.

He'd only known Lucy a few hours but he instinctively knew she'd lived her life to the full, as he had. And the quiet way she was waiting for him to begin made him think she'd suffered, too.

'You asked me about my English,' he began carefully. 'My wife's father was English. Her mother was Italian. I met Lavinia when I was working in a hospital near London. She was a theatre sister. I was working in Accident and Emergency. Our paths crossed all the time when we were working. I would be sending patients to Theatre, checking on their post-operative progress, all that sort of thing. And with Lavinia, it was, as you English say, love at first sight.'

He paused, and Lucy waited, not wanting to break the spell. All around them the sounds of evening revelry were becoming louder—laughter, music, someone playing a guitar. But here on the banks of the Tiber, this famous, ancient river, she felt they had created their own little oasis of calm.

'If only I hadn't persuaded Lavinia to leave England!'

Vittorio's words came out in an ominous rush. He took a sip of his wine, breathing deeply as he replaced the glass on the table.

Lucy felt a sense of foreboding as she witnessed the depth of Vittorio's emotions. This was going to be an awful revelation. Did she want Vittorio to go through the trauma of reliving the experience?

'If I hadn't brought Lavinia to Italy, she would still be alive,' Vittorio continued quietly.

Lucy found herself holding her breath as she waited

for Vittorio to continue, knowing instinctively, by the nuances in Vittorio's voice, that the revelations would be distressing. Seconds passed. Vittorio put the tips of his fingers against each other, bowing his head over them as if in prayer.

As he closed his eyes, willing himself to reveal the awful details of Lavinia's death to this sympathetic listener, he knew he couldn't do it. It would only bring everything back and he would feel the suffering and the pain once more. It was better to keep this secret from Lucy. He hardly knew her, so why was he even contemplating baring his soul to her?

He raised his head and looked across the table. Lucy could see the expression of anguish in his eyes. She couldn't bear to see his anguish.

'What…what happened, Vittorio?'

Vittorio swallowed hard. 'My wife…my wife died…in tragic circumstances…five years ago,' he said in a hoarse whisper. 'But I don't wish to speak about it further.'

He took a deep breath to stop himself from saying more. He was deeply tempted to elaborate, to listen to some comforting words from this new colleague. But he had to remain strong. If he described the details, the awful events surrounding that day five years ago, he would break down all his defences. He had to remain strong and silent. He didn't want to appear vulnerable in front of a colleague he hardly knew.

At first, Lucy found she couldn't speak. She wanted to reach across and hold Vittorio against her to give him some comfort. He looked so desolate. He'd spoken of tragic circumstances. Whatever those had been, the effect on Vittorio must have been devastating. Words were never sufficient at a time like this but eventually she found her voice.

'Vittorio, I'm so sorry,' she whispered in a husky voice. 'I can't imagine how—'

'It's better you don't,' Vittorio interrupted. 'Let's live in the present, shall we? I asked you out for a drink so that we could both relax at the end of our working day.'

Vittorio was making a valiant attempt to lighten the mood again, but Lucy wasn't taken in by his brave performance. What were the tragic circumstances surrounding his wife's death?

She took a sip of wine as she realised that Vittorio wasn't going to answer the questions that were tumbling through her mind. She would have to be content with the bare facts that he'd told her…for the present. It was tragic enough that his wife had died but that there was some other dimension to the tragedy made it all the more poignant. She could see that whatever had happened had radically changed Vittorio's life.

Lucy cleared her throat. 'Vittorio…words can't convey my sadness at what you've suffered, but I hope in some way that by telling me just now…'

Vittorio reached for her hand and again pressed it to his lips. In the five years since Lavinia had died he'd never found anyone who'd shown him such empathy. Not sympathy. He didn't want sympathy. But Lucy knew exactly how to put herself in the shoes of someone who'd suffered. And he was grateful.

When he'd asked her out this evening, he hadn't known why. It was his usual response to a beautiful woman who seemed lively and interesting. He'd done this so many times in the last five years. After the tragedy of Lavinia he knew he'd never be able to risk loving and losing again. He daren't commit himself emotionally to another relationship and risk having his heart broken.

Asking Lucy to come for a drink this evening had been a spur-of-the-moment idea. He hadn't wanted to be alone.

'Why don't you tell me something about yourself, Lucy? What made you give up your job in England?'

Lucy hesitated. 'That's also a long story,' she said carefully as the memories of the past year came rushing back. 'Let's just say that I had a disastrous relationship. If I give you the details I'll...' She checked the sob that rose in her throat as the anger and sadness threatened to engulf her again. 'No, I'd rather not talk about it.'

Vittorio stood up and came round the table, leaning down to put his arm around her shoulders.

'I think I recognise a fellow sufferer,' he whispered as he bent his head and brushed her cheek with his lips.

Lucy looked up. Vittorio's lips were hovering above hers. She raised her head and kissed him, slowly, deliberately, sensually.

Vittorio put out his hands and cupped her face in his. Gently he kissed her again, keeping his eyes open to test her reaction. Here was a warm, vibrant woman who'd suffered as he had. He didn't know what had happened to her but her pain was blatant. A night of pure sensual pleasure would be therapeutic for both of them, so long as they didn't find themselves becoming too emotionally involved.

But something was holding him back. Lucy was different. Lucy was somehow special. With Lucy he recognised that holding onto his emotions wasn't going to be possible. He was already bonding with her in a way that could prove dangerous.

Lucy resolved the situation by standing up. The magic spell was broken for both of them.

'I need to get back to the hospital,' she said quickly. 'I promised my sister I would go to see her and baby Charlotte again this evening.'

Vittorio put his hands on either side of her shoulders and stood looking down into her beautiful blue eyes. He knew perfectly well that, because he found Lucy so attractive, it would be dangerous to meet with her again, but he was trying to convince himself that he could stay emotionally independent. Trying to tell himself that it would be possible to spend time with such a charismatic woman and not fall in love with her.

'Perhaps we could have supper together soon,' he found himself saying. I have a feeling you've led an interesting life and—'

'I need time to settle in,' Lucy said quickly as she recognised the signs that she was finding this handsome Italian far too attractive.

The last thing she needed was romantic complications in her life! Never again! Mark had seemed so attractive, so utterly trustworthy, so desirable. And she'd fallen for him, hook line and sinker. And the consequences had been diabolical. A year later she should have recovered, but she hadn't. And she wasn't going to go down that road again, even though she fancied Vittorio rotten!

Vittorio smiled. He felt almost relieved that Lucy was playing hard to get. True, she'd instigated that kiss and he might have been tempted to think she was attracted to him. But she was making it perfectly clear that she was no pushover, especially in a physical sense!

'Well, when you've settled in, maybe I could ask you

out for supper one evening?' he asked in his most polite, perfect English voice.

'Yes, I would enjoy that,' Lucy said, thankful that Vittorio couldn't detect the loud thumping of her heart.

CHAPTER TWO

IT WAS a whole week before Vittorio decided it might be appropriate to invite Lucy to go out for supper with him. He'd lain awake during the night after they'd had a drink together, wondering what it was that was so special about this woman. What was it about her personality that had affected him so much? It wasn't as if he was looking to find this sort of response from a woman. Especially one he'd only known for a day.

He'd reflected on the fact that he'd felt deeply aroused after he'd dropped her off outside the obstetric ward. He'd wanted to suggest to Lucy that he meet her again after she'd seen her sister. But he would have been demoralised if she'd turned him down, which was a real possibility because she was a feisty, independent sort of person.

The arrival of Lucy, seeing her every day in hospital, had thrown him completely. But he'd no idea what it was he wanted where Lucy was concerned. He was playing a dangerous game by allowing himself to dwell on the fact that he was magnetically drawn to her. He was trying desperately to convince himself that he could go out again with Lucy and remain emotionally detached. So long as they simply had a light-hearted evening together, all he wanted was to enjoy her company for a few hours.

Would he be able to do that? Keep a tight rein on his emotions and simply take Lucy out for a good time? Of course he could, if he remained cool! He'd given no indications of his feelings when they were working together, had he?

At the end of a week of trying to be completely professional with Lucy, it was only after much soul-searching that he went into Pronto Soccorso early so that he would have time for a chat with Lucy. He'd discovered that she was always in very early because she liked to check on what was happening to the patients she'd admitted to the primary care units.

He arrived just in time to see her disappearing down the corridor. It would have been unprofessional to call out her name, so he followed her along the corridor, quickly catching up with her.

Taking a deep breath, he asked if she was free that evening.

Lucy looked up at Vittorio in surprise. They'd worked together for the past week but had hardly exchanged more than a few words that hadn't been related to their work.

'What did you have in mind?'

Vittorio gave Lucy a long slow languid smile that utterly belied the emotional turmoil going on inside him. He was trying to remain calm. He'd done this so often, asked a lovely girl out for supper, so why was this proving to be so important and so difficult for him?

'I'd like to spend the evening with you. When we were at Giovanni's you began to tell me something about your life. I hoped you might tell me something more over supper tonight at a restaurant?'

Lucy raised an eyebrow. 'I'm a very simple soul.'

Vittorio leaned forward and put both hands on her shoulders. 'I don't think so. You're the most complicated character I've met in a long time.'

She looked up into his eyes, enjoying the excitement

she saw in his expression. During the last week whenever she'd met him he'd appeared more invigorated. Unwillingly, she'd like to think that she'd helped him in some small way to get over his trauma. But at the same time she recognised that she was becoming too attracted to Vittorio. Much too attracted.

Once bitten, twice shy. She couldn't afford the emotional trauma of going down that road again. But if she played it cool and didn't become emotionally involved...

'OK, I'll tell you some of my life story over supper. But not much. It might spoil your digestion.'

She was being deliberately facetious, making it absolutely clear that this was simply an evening when they would relax and take it easy. Nothing heavy!

Vittorio laughed. Lucy had never heard him laugh before Never seen him look remotely happy. What was happening to both of them? She daren't even think about it. Instinctively she held her breath.

'I shall look forward to out evening together,' he said lightly.

The evening, he told himself firmly. He did not intend to ask Lucy if she would like to go to bed with him. He did not want to classify her with the other women who'd given him a brief respite from his misery in the oblivion of a sexual encounter. Lucy was different. He had no idea how he intended the evening to end but it certainly wasn't in bed. He simply wanted to spend time with her. Get to know her. Get to know what made her tick, to use that strange English phrase.

Well, that was what he was telling himself! Whether he could abide by his own rules was a different matter. Sexual temptation was a difficult thing to resist, especially with a woman as sensually attractive as Lucy.

'I'll meet you in Reception when we come off duty, Lucy,' Vittorio said in a confident voice, feeling the least self-assurance he'd known for a long time.

Lucy had shown him compassion and empathy when he'd told her that Lavinia had died in tragic circumstances. He'd never known such comfort. She hadn't pitied him. She'd instinctively understood the situation. Even though he'd given her no details, she'd felt empathy for him. But empathy and compassion were quite different to the way he'd felt for her during the past week.

Lucy smiled. 'I insist on changing my clothes this time. I felt so dishevelled in comparison with all the chic Italian girls in Enotecca Giovanni.'

Vittorio leaned forward and put one hand under her chin, tilting her lovely, radiant face upwards.

'Clothes are unimportant,' he said, in a deep, husky, sexy voice. 'Just be there this evening…with me.'

On the surface Lucy appeared cool as Vittorio walked on, leaving her standing in the middle of the corridor.

Vittorio had walked away as quickly as possible because he was losing his grip! Losing his concentration. Wanting the day to be over so that he could meet up again with this gorgeous creature. But it was a long time until this evening and he needed to stay focused on his work. Talking to Lucy had been too much of a distraction. He wasn't supposed to feel so attracted to her.

He rammed a hand against his forehead. *Mamma mia!* He was only taking a woman out for supper. That's all it was! No need for all this soul-searching! But if it was so unimportant an event, why was he feeling so…so different, so alive, so…?

It was because he was allowing Lucy to break through his emotional barrier. And he mustn't allow that to happen. He must never allow himself to fall in love again. Because he couldn't risk the trauma of being in love and losing the object of his love. He wouldn't let that happen. He would cling to his emotional independence.

He swallowed hard as he turned the corridor and pushed open the swing doors leading to Orthopaedics. The orthopaedic team was waiting for him to make a difficult decision about whether to amputate or try to save a badly smashed leg. He had to be one hundred per cent committed to his work for the rest of the day. His orthopaedic patients mustn't suffer because he was spending too much time thinking about a certain woman doctor.

Lucy watched as Vittorio rounded the corner before she moved swiftly into the paediatrics ward. She wasn't going to allow herself to think about the impact that her meeting with Vittorio had made on her. She'd made a point of being totally professional whenever they'd worked together since they'd shared a bottle of wine together at Giovanni Enotecca. And until she'd met Vittorio this morning she'd thought she had her emotions under control.

But seeing him just now, in his relaxed, devastatingly suggestive mood, she wasn't sure she would be able to hold out if he came on strong this evening.

He's only asked me out for supper, for heaven's sake! But she'd recognised the sexual signals passing between them…the rapport that was springing up. She'd known on that first evening that their mutual experiences had brought them closer. Closer than was safe if she wanted to remain emotionally independent for the foreseeable future. It was too soon after her disastrous relationship with Mark to be feeling like this.

It was a well-known fact that disillusioned women were vulnerable for a long time after they'd been let down. And the danger of falling for somebody on the rebound was ever present and something she needed to guard against.

As she went into Paediatrics, she made a deliberate effort to blank out her own personal thoughts as she walked over to her little patient's bed. Six-year-old Roberta, the child who'd come into Pronto Soccorso a week ago with a high temperature, vomiting and pain in the right iliac fossa, was sitting on top of her sheets, reading a book. She looked up and smiled as she saw Lucy arriving at her bedside. Closing the book, she began chattering quickly in her childish but very clear and easy-to-understand Italian.

During the non-stop chatter, Roberta told Lucy that her tummy didn't hurt any more. Only if she moved quickly and pulled on the stitches. She'd made lots of friends here in the hospital but when could she go home to her mummy?

Lucy sat down at the side of the bed and listened to the chatter, smiling and nodding, adding a few words here and there. Glancing at the notes, she saw that the surgeon who'd performed the appendectomy a week ago was extremely pleased with Roberta's progress. But the drainage tube had only just been removed so he was going to keep their patient in hospital for a few more days to make sure that there was no danger of further complications.

'I think you'll be fit to go home next weekend, Roberta,' Lucy said, patting the little girl's hand. 'Has your mummy been in to see you?'

Roberta smiled happily. 'Yes, she comes in every afternoon. Will you come in to see me again, Lucy?'

'Of course.'

Lucy settled herself easily in the chair at the side of the bed. In the early morning, before she started work, she made a point of following up as many of the patients she'd admitted as possible. She'd always done this because otherwise there was no continuity and less satisfaction in her job. Sometimes she was called away to an emergency as soon as she arrived at the hospital. But today had been relatively quiet—so far!

She had two more patients to see, if she could fit them in before work. She found that Alfredo Fontana, the man who'd fallen from his balcony and suffered a fractured skull, was still unconscious. His devoted wife, Anastasia, was just waking up in the chair at his bedside in the intensive care unit. She gave Lucy a bleak smile devoid of any warmth.

'How much longer before Alfredo regains consciousness, Lucy?'

'I really couldn't say, Anastasia,' Lucy said as she glanced at Alfredo's notes. 'We're doing everything we can. The operation to remove the large blood clot that was pressing on the brain was a success so we shall just have to be patient. The brain is like a complex piece of machinery. Alfredo could come round from his coma at any time. There's no clinical reason why not.'

Lucy swallowed hard. She wasn't going to add to Anastasia's worries by saying that some patients in her husband's condition never regained consciousness. The consultant had spelt it all out to the young woman in the days following Alfredo's operation. Anastasia knew the score even though she was trying to be optimistic—as indeed Lucy herself was. Alfredo had everything to live for and his death would be such a waste of a young life.

In the final few minutes available Lucy went to see

Cecilia. Her fractured ribs were less painful but the discharge from her cracked right nipple had proved to be carcinogenic. She was scheduled for surgery that morning.

'What exactly are they going to do to me today?' Cecilia asked as she stared up at Lucy.

Lucy saw that her patient had already been prepared for Theatre and was first on the list. She'd discussed the case with the surgeon the previous day. She knew that he'd spent a long time explaining all the implications to their patient but it didn't do any harm to reinforce the information. Cecilia had been given the full facts about the cancer so that she would be fully prepared for any eventuality.

'The surgeon is going to make an investigative exploration of your right breast,' Lucy said carefully. 'There's a deep-seated tumour there which will have to be removed. Your surgeon has recommended a mastectomy. At the same time as the mastectomy he will reconstruct the breast with skin and muscle taken from your back, plus an implant. Now, your surgeon has stressed that the prognosis is good because we've caught this early.'

Cecilia nodded resignedly. 'I'm glad you detected that discharge coming out of my nipple, Lucy. I'd had it for some time but I didn't feel it was important, given that I couldn't feel a lump or anything. What would have happened if I'd left it?'

'The cancer would have been much harder to deal with if we'd left it any longer. As it is, we've caught it early so you should make a good recovery.'

Lucy patted Cecilia's hand. 'Giving an accurate prognosis is always a hard thing to do, but modern-day surgery is literally working miracles.'

'Thank you so much, Lucy. You've given me such hope for the future.'

Lucy's day in Pronto Soccorso started slowly. Rome was only just coming alive. But by midmorning the assessment area was humming with activity. There had been a train derailment just outside Rome and some of the casualties had been brought into the Ospedale Tevere.

She spent a large part of the day dealing with broken bones, taking patients to the plaster room for their bones to be set or taking them to Theatre for manipulative surgery. Then there were the cases of minor cuts that had to be sutured, wounds that had to be dressed, crying children who had to be matched up with the right parents.

An elderly lady was brought in unconscious. The paramedics suspected she'd had a heart attack but when Lucy began to resuscitate her she opened her eyes, looked around her and asked, in English, for a cup of tea. She said she had no recollection of being on a train and no idea who she was. The only thing she was sure of was that a cup of tea would restore her to normality.

Obviously very relieved that Lucy understood what she was talking about, the patient clung to her hand.

'When's my tea coming, Doctor?'

'It's on its way. You'll be taken to X-ray soon and then you'll be going to a bed in our primary medical unit. Now, are you sure you can't remember your name?'

'Can't remember a thing except— Ah, that's lovely, dear.' The elderly lady took the cup of tea from the nurse.

Lucy asked the nurse to take her patient to X-Ray as

soon as she'd finished her tea. Then she moved on to the next patient.

It was early evening before Lucy had time to check up on the elderly lady brought in after the train crash. She found her sitting up in bed, drinking another cup of tea and complaining that you couldn't get a decent cup of tea outside England.

Lucy took hold of her patient's hand. The skin was cold, dry and wrinkled. The lady could be any age between seventy and eighty-five. The apparent amnaesia was something of a mystery because there was no sign of injury to the head.

'How are you feeling now?' Lucy said.

'Not too bad now. I don't know why they took me for that X-ray. There's nothing wrong with my head. And then they put me through another machine and still they couldn't find what's wrong with me.'

'You still can't remember who you are?' Lucy asked gently.

The elderly patient giggled. 'I might be the queen of England for all you know. Call me Queenie just in case.'

Lucy smiled. 'Shall I tell the other medical staff that's your name?'

'Why not, dear?'

Lucy began scribbling in the notes. 'And shall I put your age as about...what shall we say? Sixty-five?'

'I shall be eighty in September, dear. My daughter's going to do a big party for me and— Oops!'

Queenie broke off and watched Lucy warily.

Lucy smiled. 'You're getting your memory back, aren't you, Queenie?'

Queenie looked around her cautiously, leaned forward and whispered, 'Actually, don't tell anybody but I never lost it. I was having a lovely sleep on the train. I woke up to find a nice young man putting me on a stretcher. I think I was enjoying all the fuss so I just kept my eyes closed. You don't get much excitement at my age.'

Lucy patted her patient's hand. 'So what shall I call you now?'

'I really am called Queenie. You'd better let my daughter know where I am. I live with her and her Italian husband just outside Rome. I must have left my handbag on the train but I can remember my daughter's number. I'll give it to you and you can phone her if you'll be so kind. And while you're on your feet, dear, could you see if you can get me a proper cup of tea? Not like this rubbish. Get them to boil the water…'

Lucy went off to explain Queenie's situation to the sister in charge of the primary medical unit. After that she went into the unit's kitchen and asked the ward maid to be sure to boil the water for Queenie's tea. Then she went back to her small office and phoned the number Queenie had given her.

Queenie's daughter was relieved to hear that her mother was safe and well. She explained that her mother sometimes wandered off without telling anybody where she was going.

'We'd no idea she was on a train. I'd only gone to the shops for a few minutes. When I got back she wasn't there. Mum used to be an actress and she sometimes goes off into a world of her own. If she can play a starring role in a drama she'll pull out all the stops! I'll come and see her now. Will I be able to bring her home with me?'

'We'd like to keep your mother in for a couple of day's observation as a routine measure. Just to make sure she's completely recovered.'

Her door opened. Lucy motioned to Vittorio to sit down.

'I won't be long. I'm just speaking to some relatives about—' She broke off as she listened to what Queenie's daughter was saying.

'Yes, by all means. Our gerontology specialist is coming to see your mother this evening. He's very kind and considerate, used to dealing with the difficult problems of the older patient... Yes, I'm sure his approach will be very subtle. Quite a character, your mother!'

'You can say that again!' was the response at the other end of the line. 'I love her to bits but she can be such a handful! I've had four children but they were easy compared to Mother.'

'I understand what you mean,' Lucy said.

Vittorio was getting impatient. 'You're late,' he whispered. 'I was waiting for you in Reception.'

As he leaned across the desk to point to his watch, she felt the brush of his sleeve against her arm. At the same time she detected the tantalising aroma of his aftershave.

'I'll have to go now,' she told Queenie's daughter. 'You'll find your mother in the primary medical unit next to Accident and Emergency.'

'Thanks very much for all you've done, Doctor.'

Lucy cut the connection and looked across the desk at Vittorio.

'Stop worrying, Lucy.' Vittorio smiled into her eyes and she felt her legs going weak.

She told herself it was because she'd been working hard all day that she was feeling so vulnerable.

'We have an excellent record in care for the elderly at the hospital. Our specialist will follow up your case now,' Vittorio said. 'How did you find out that the old lady was called Queenie?'

Lucy smiled. 'She hadn't really lost her memory. She told me she was enjoying the fuss and the excitement. She's a dear old soul.'

Vittorio stood up and came round to Lucy's side of the desk. 'Come on, I'm going to take you out of here now.'

'I'd prefer to shower and change first.'

Vittorio groaned. 'You look fine.'

'I don't feel fine. Next time we go out together I'll make a point of leaving early enough.'

Lucy made for the door quickly as she realised what she'd just said. Was she making it apparent that she hoped they would go out again? In spite of having told herself she wouldn't become too involved, her heart was already beating madly. What would she be like by the end of the evening?

It was the sort of evening when young couples who'd been working all day came out for a stroll in the cooling temperatures after the intense heat of the day. On their way to the restaurant, Lucy and Vittorio sat for a while at the edge of the Trevi fountains, watching the spray of the water, its droplets appearing strikingly iridescent in the dying rays of the evening sun.

'It's so relaxing, just doing nothing,' Lucy said, as she trailed her hand in the water. 'Pretending to be a tourist.'

'Instead of a working girl,' Vittorio said, taking hold of her hand as she lifted it out of the water. 'Your tiny hand is frozen…just like Mimi's in the opera La Bohème.'

Vittorio removed a clean white linen handkerchief

from his pocket and began wiping her wet hand, slowly stroking each finger.

'I love that aria where Mimi meets her lover for the first time,' Lucy said quickly.

She needed to keep talking to cover up the fact that the movement of his hand over hers was much too disturbing. 'That bit where Rudolpho tells Mimi that her hand is cold and—'

'*Que gelida manina…*' Vittorio sang softly under his breath as he continued to stroke her hand long after it was already dry.

Lucy swallowed hard. Even though Vittorio was singing very quietly, she could tell he had an excellent tenor voice. It was so romantic, sitting here by the fountains with a handsome Italian who seemed to be paying her far more attention than either of them had planned.

Vittorio pushed the handkerchief into his trouser pocket but continued to hold her hand.

'Do you like opera, Lucy?'

She noticed that Vittorio's speaking voice was now husky, sexy, decidedly appealing. All around them couples were strolling about, sitting by the fountains, chattering, laughing, oblivious to the rest of the crowd. And just like she and Vittorio, they seemed only to have eyes for each other.

I'm not falling in love, she told herself firmly as she struggled to get a grip on her feelings. It was the romantic atmosphere of a summer evening in Rome that was affecting her. Being surrounded by couples openly displaying their affection for each other. But as she raised her eyes to Vittorio's she knew she was steadily being drawn by some magnetic force into the magic spell that Vittorio, consciously or unconsciously, was weaving around her.

'Yes, I love opera, Vittorio,' she said quietly.

He smiled. 'Good. Will you come to the opera with me one evening?'

'Only if I have time to change first!'

Vittorio laughed. 'I will personally see to it that you leave early. Now, let's go and have some supper. But first you must make a wish by the fountains.'

He pulled some coins from his pocket and tossed them into the water.

'My sister told me she made a wish here and it came true,' Lucy said softly.

'Never fails…or so I'm told. So close your eyes and wish, Lucy.'

She closed her eyes but her thoughts were too confused to make a coherent wish. If she allowed her head to make the decision it would be easy. But if she went with her heart and even considered some of the outrageously romantic notions that were running through her head…

She opened her eyes as the light touch of Vittorio's lips on her cheek startled and excited her.

'I couldn't resist that! I was merely awakening the sleeping beauty from her sleep, like somebody did in that old fairy tale my mother used to read to me when I was a boy.'

'Prince Charming, let's go!' she said lightly.

Vittorio took hold of Lucy's hand. It was as if they were living in a complete make-believe world. The cares of the day were all behind them and they were simply a couple of friends out to have fun.

Friends! That was the relationship her head told her to maintain. Anything else was asking for trouble. Although, as she slipped her fingers through Vittorio's, Lucy thought she might be able to let down her guard a little this evening. Just for a few hours... She needn't get carried away by the romantic atmosphere of Rome and the fact that the Prince Charming beside her was everything she could ever wish for...if she'd happened to have made such an irresponsible wish.

Which, of course, she hadn't! Well, she'd tried her hardest not to...

The restaurant was crowded but Vittorio had reserved a table by the window. Starched white tablecloth and napkins, sparkling glasses reflecting the flickering of the candles.

Vittorio ordered a bottle of wine as they studied the menu. Lucy chose artichokes as her starter. They were a speciality that always reminded her of one of the happy times when she'd been in Rome with her family as a child.

'I was about five when I first ate artichokes,' Lucy said. 'I didn't imagine I would like them but I've been hooked on them ever since. Especially when I'm in Italy. Some kind of nostalgia, I suppose. I had a happy childhood.'

'So did I,' Vittorio said as he speared a couple of anchovies onto his fork. 'My seafood starter is seriously good.'

Almost without a break from the subject of their meal, he began asking Lucy about her adult life.

'What happened after your childhood? You went to medical school and then what?'

'You're fishing for information about my love life, aren't you? You don't fool me, Vittorio.'

He grinned. 'Not necessarily. Anything interesting that happened when you were an adult. Boyfriends, yes, if you want to tell me.'

'So many I can't remember! And how about the girl-friends you enticed as a teenager? Now it's your turn.'

'A constant supply of beautiful girls!'

They were both laughing now. Maybe it was a combination of the wine, the convivial atmosphere, the lack of responsibility as they sat at their table, simply enjoying themselves.

Lucy ate *saltimbocca alla Romana*, veal with Parma ham and sage, which was delicious.

'Excellent,' she said as she put down her fork, unable to eat any more. Vittorio finished his fillet steak and then insisted she try the tiramisu which was another speciality at the restaurant.

As they sat drinking coffee, Lucy realised that their conversation had ranged over a variety of subjects—films, music, theatre, books—but apart from the facetious reference to boyfriends and girlfriends they hadn't touched on anything personal that might be upsetting. They'd both been deliberately steering clear of the serious aspects of their adult lives that had been life-changing.

'So, are you going to tell me about the love rat you mentioned last time we went out together?'

Vittorio's words cut through her thoughts as if he'd been mind-reading.

'Mark, his name was Mark,' Lucy began, absently picking up her spoon and stirring her coffee. 'That was the name he first gave me and I had no reason to question that it wasn't his real name…at the time.'

She glanced up at Vittorio who was staring at her, wide-eyed. 'But why would he want to give you a false name?'

'Because he didn't want me to be able to trace who he really was. In effect he was nothing but a con man.

But unfortunately I thought I'd fallen in love with him…in fact, I had fallen in love with him. But not the man he really was. Not the false, conniving…'

Vittorio put his hand across the table and covered her fingers to stop her from trembling.

'Don't upset yourself. Look, if you'd rather not talk about it…'

'I want to tell you, Vittorio. There's so much anger stored up inside me. It would be a good release of tension, I think. I just don't know where to begin.'

Vittorio leaned back in his chair. 'I'm listening. Why don't you start at the beginning?'

'Mark told me he was an airline pilot and I believed him. He said he sometimes had to fly into Newcastle airport. I met him on a train when I was on my way to Newcastle for a medical conference. He told me he was flying out that day but he asked if he could call me next time he was back in the UK. We met infrequently at first. He told me he was divorced. His wife had remarried and lived in the USA.'

'And all this was untrue?'

Lucy gave a harsh laugh. 'A complete fabrication. He was actually a customs officer based at Newcastle. He had a wife and two children. When I discovered all this, his wife was pregnant with their third child.'

She swallowed hard. That was one of the bits of this painful story that hurt the most. The fact that Mark's wife had been pregnant around the same time that she herself had fallen pregnant. But his wife's pregnancy continued successfully, whereas she herself had miscarried only days before she'd found out the truth about him. But that was the part of the story she didn't want to discuss with Vittorio. Not tonight when they'd been having such fun. She planned to give him the shortened version.

'How did you find out the truth?'

'Quite by chance. I had to meet a friend who was flying into Newcastle. I was waiting around in Arrivals when who should come sauntering through but Mark. Not in an airline pilot's uniform but dressed as a customs officer.'

'Did he see you?'

'No. I don't expect he ever thought I'd be at the airport. I live miles away in the Yorkshire Dales. If ever I fly off anywhere, it's usually from Manchester or Leeds, sometimes London. In the year that Mark and I were together I hadn't flown anywhere. Like an idiot, I'd work all day in hospital, return to my cottage in the Dales at night and wait for him to phone. Even when I was on holiday from the hospital I stayed in England, checking my answering-machine every day in case I needed to hurry home.'

'You must have really loved him.'

'Oh, I did! I loved who I thought was Mark. He used to keep some of his clothes at my cottage. When he asked me to marry him, I agreed wholeheartedly. I had no reason to suspect the truth. He had such plans for our future. He said he was due to be promoted soon. He was going to take a top salaried administrative job where he would be based in London. He was going to buy an expensive house for us in the south. It was only a question of time before…'

She broke off, waited a few seconds before she was in control again. 'Looking back, I realise what a fool I was. Falling in love is so dangerous! You lose all your sense of reason and you behave as if—'

'But you were dealing with an accomplished con man

who was not only cheating on you but cheating on his wife. That was unforgivable of him. No man should cheat on his wife. Being faithful to the family is the most important thing in life!'

Vittorio squeezed her hand. 'What happened on the day you saw him at the airport?'

'I went into a state of shock! I couldn't believe what I was seeing. The airport was very crowded. He passed so close to me. I could have spoken to him at the time but I didn't want to make a scene there. I spent an agonising week trying to sort out my feelings, planning what I should do. When he turned up about a week later at the cottage, saying that he'd just flown in from Barbados, I challenged him.'

She took a sip of the strong black coffee before looking across the table at Vittorio. Her eyes were moist and misty as she tried to withhold some of the emotion she was feeling.

'Did he explain?' Vittorio asked, his voice husky.

'Not at first. At first he tried to bluff it out, said I must have been mistaken. I was still hoping that maybe I had been. Maybe there was a reason why he wasn't a pilot any more. All sorts of childish notions…'

'So how long was it before…?'

'After a few minutes of continuing the deception, he suddenly broke down. Started crying. Saying he'd been going to tell me everything. He hadn't meant to keep up the pretence for so long. Hadn't meant to ask me to marry him because he was already married. He'd only meant to keep up the pretence for a few weeks. Then he found he didn't want to stop seeing me. But now it was all becoming too complicated for him.'

'I asked if his wife knew about me. He said no, but she was pregnant with their third child and he knew he would have to spend more time with her. It had been worrying him. His wife was becoming suspicious of the times he stayed at the cottage. He'd had to make up all sorts of lies about having to work in another area of the country but she was beginning to ask too many questions. He would move his stuff out of the cottage and he wouldn't come to see me again.'

'How did his explanation make you feel?'

'Used! Like an old shoe, a discarded garment. Something of no worth at all.'

'You poor girl!' Vittorio whispered.

As Lucy stared at the dark brown eyes that showed Vittorio was so concerned, so full of sympathy, she felt a certain easing of her pain.

'Let's leave now,' Vittorio said gently. 'We'll go for a walk through the streets, down to the river. You can tell me some more as we walk and—'

'Yes, I'd like to walk, but I don't want to talk about it any more. I want to leave it all in the past and move on.'

Vittorio nodded as he called for the bill. 'I know what you mean. If only it was that easy.'

'You understand, don't you, Vittorio?'

'Yes…I understand perfectly'

They held hands as they walked through the darkened streets, down to the twinkling lights by the river. Their conversation was once again on neutral subjects.

They discussed music, especially opera and those operas they would like to see and hear again. To Lucy it was as if she'd discovered a kindred spirit, someone who understood what she'd been through—or thought he did.

The break-up of what she'd imagined to be the love of her life had been bad enough, but the miscarriage of the precious baby she'd so desperately wanted was something she wasn't strong enough to discuss with Vittorio.

She'd never told anybody, not even Sarah, about her miscarriage or the necessary operation that had followed. The operation that had removed the remnants of her pregnancy, that might have left post-operative complications which would prevent her from becoming pregnant again.

They were nearing the hospital. The lights were dimmed in the wards but Pronto Soccorso was fully illuminated. An ambulance was arriving. Doors were being opened. Night staff were hurrying out to check on the new arrival.

'Let's go round the back to avoid getting involved,' Vittorio said. 'There's a side entrance to the residents' quarters that I sometimes use. Would you like to come to my room for a drink? What do you call it in England? Ah, yes, a nightcap. Strange expression!'

Vittorio was talking quickly, being as impersonal as he could. It wasn't easy, given the quickening of his heart as he looked down at Lucy. She looked so beautiful and so vulnerable. He knew it wasn't wise to invite her back to his room but he couldn't help himself. He'd tried to sound so casual but he found he was holding his breath as he waited for her reply.

Lucy was weighing up the pros and cons. Her head was telling her to go straight to her room. A late-night rendezvous with a handsome man whose charming company she'd enjoyed all evening was the sort of venture she should avoid. She'd made such a fool of herself with Mark. Who was to say that Vittorio was exactly who he said he was? Shouldn't she wait until she'd known him a bit longer? Shouldn't she...?

'I'd love to!' The words were out before she could stop them.

She looked sideways at his profile in the moonlight and thought she detected an expression of relief on his face. Maybe Vittorio had been agonising over whether he should invite her to his room or not. Having loved his wife as he had, maybe he was trying to stay faithful to her memory and wondering if it was wrong to spend time with another woman.

So both of them had every reason to make this simply a drink at the end of an enjoyable evening out together. No emotion, nothing heavy, she told herself as she followed Vittorio to his room.

CHAPTER THREE

VITTORIO closed the door behind them.

'Vittorio, may I use your bathroom?'

'Of course. It's the door on the right.'

'Thank you.'

Oh, they were both being so polite with each other! As Lucy hurried across the room she was feeling decidedly nervous. The easy, friendly, positively romantic rapport that had been with them ever since they'd sat beside the Trevi fountains had been dissipated by the mere fact that they were now two people alone with all the hidden implications and possibilities the situation now presented.

As Lucy closed the bathroom door she knew she shouldn't have given in to the temptation of spending more time with Vittorio. She should have gone straight to her room, safe from doing something she might regret.

Vittorio remained motionless as he watched Lucy walking over to the bathroom. He leaned against the door, wondering what on earth had possessed him to invite her into his room. What would she be expecting? What was he hoping would happen? Of course he wanted to make love to her. But that was just his primeval sexual instinct coming to the fore.

But Lucy was different. Lucy was special. One false move on his part and he could shatter the close friendship that was building up between them. And that was all he wanted. A no-strings-attached friendship with someone who intrigued and interested him. A touch of romance perhaps? Of course! Exactly what they had at the moment. Anything more would be too emotionally dangerous to contemplate.

He walked slowly into his little kitchen, deliberating all the time about how he should handle the next few minutes. He'd never felt like this before about a woman. With Lavinia it had been young love, love at first sight, leaping into bed at the first opportunity. No past to regret or long for, no mistakes made in previous relationships, no past, no future, just the free glorious innocence of youth.

And with all the casual flings he'd settled for since Lavinia's death he'd merely sought some sexual release that had been mutually satisfying to both himself and his partner of the moment, uncomplicated, uncommitted, devoid of emotion.

But that wasn't what he wanted to happen with Lucy. And somehow he instinctively knew it wasn't what she wanted either. Tonight, as she'd told him how she'd been duped by that love rat, he'd found himself longing to get his hands on the man who'd devastated her life. It was as if he was now personally involved in what happened to Lucy.

He'd love to know more details about how exactly this duplicitous man had deceived Lucy and in what ways she'd had to suffer. But she obviously didn't want to tell him. Any more than he himself felt he could divulge the details of the tragic day he'd lost his family. Neither could he bear to voice the other, poignant secret in his life which was always there to taunt and sadden him.

Although he could tell that Lucy was tough in some ways, in others she seemed like a tender young plant that needed to be shielded from harm.

He pulled open the fridge door, leaning against it as he surveyed the contents. There was a bottle of champagne waiting to be uncorked. Would Lucy think he was trying to seduce her? More to the point, *was* he trying to seduce her? He was trying not to but…

He lifted the bottle out of the fridge. It was an expensive vintage, waiting for a special occasion. He'd invited Lucy in for a nightcap so only the best would do. That was his motivation, he told himself, and began to feel relieved that he'd managed to make one decision out of the jumbled ideas that were tumbling through his head.

'A glass of champagne, Lucy?'

He was trying to sound as if he routinely drank vintage champagne every night of the week as he carried the bottle and a couple of glasses into his living room.

'Why not?' Lucy said, trying desperately to lighten up. 'Thank you very much.'

She took the glass he was holding out and decided she would have one glass and then she would leave before she began to feel too mellow and lost control of the situation.

He clinked his glass against hers. She smiled up into his dark brown eyes and felt a momentary flicker of excitement running down her spine. Don't let me fall in love with Vittorio, she was saying inwardly to whatever inner force was in charge of keeping a check on her emotions. I don't want to make a repeat performance of the awful mistakes I made with Mark. I'm not going to let down my guard, not even for someone as drop-dead gorgeous as Vittorio…especially someone as drop-dead gorgeous as Vittorio!

She crossed one leg over the other and straightened her back against the squashy cushions of the sofa as she sipped her champagne. Vittorio sat down at the other end of the large sofa.

'You're nervous, aren't you, Lucy?' he asked.

'Nervous? Why should I be nervous?'

'Perhaps because you're alone with me? There's no need...'

'No, I'm perfectly at ease here with you, Vittorio.'

She meant to take another sip but drank a large gulp instead, and the sudden influx of the champagne into her throat made her begin to cough and splutter.

'I'm sorry! I...'

She put down her glass on the coffee-table at the side of the sofa. The glass fell over and champagne poured out over the table and onto the carpet.

'Oh, no! I didn't mean to ruin your carpet. Let me—'

'Don't worry, Lucy. Champagne doesn't stain.' Vittorio removed the handkerchief with which he'd dried Lucy's hands from his pocket and dabbed at the carpet. 'Good as new. Let me get you a fresh glass. No, I insist.'

Lucy had stopped spluttering. Vittorio moved along the sofa and, taking Lucy's glass from her hands, put it safely on the coffee-table. Turning round, he drew her into the circle of his arms. Gently, he lowered his head and kissed her on the lips. Ah, he'd wanted to do this so much all evening!

He could feel every fibre of his being longing to make love to her. And that was precisely why he knew he had to call a halt before he allowed himself to give in to his natural instincts. Feeling as he did at the moment, he knew he couldn't hold Lucy in his arms any longer and remain emotionally detached.

It wouldn't be possible to have a romantic encounter of a sexual nature with Lucy without losing his heart to her. And that was something he was never going to do ever again. He was never going to leave himself wide open to the anguish he'd suffered by losing the family he'd worshipped.

He pulled himself away and took a deep breath.

Lucy glanced across at Vittorio, surprised by his sudden change of mood. She'd felt deeply aroused by the touch of his lips as she'd nestled into the warmth of his embrace. She'd longed to go further, to lose herself in the excitement of being with a man as vibrant and sensually charismatic as Vittorio, but at the same time she knew this wouldn't have made sense.

Where emotional involvement was concerned she'd been a complete disaster! She'd been too trusting in the past. She'd accepted people at face value. And from the deep-down feeling she had at the moment, she was in terrible danger of falling in love again.

'It's time I escorted you back to your room,' Vittorio said firmly, his hooded eyes matching the darkly brooding expression on his face.

Lucy suppressed the sigh that sprang to her lips. Vittorio was once again the enigmatic, mysterious man she'd first encountered in Carlos's office. He'd opened up briefly to her, but now he was clamping down again.

What had she learned about him in the short time she'd known him? That he'd lost his wife in tragic circumstances. He'd hinted that there was even more tragedy in his life, but she didn't feel he would ever divulge his secrets to her. He seemed strangely mixed up from an emotional point of view.

But, above all, she knew that she was too deeply attracted to him to count him as a casual friend. If Vittorio had suggested they go into his bedroom tonight, she wouldn't have hesitated. Her whole body was tingling with longing for him.

So, yes, it was definitely time she left! Vittorio was standing in front of her, holding out his hand. She took it, trying to ignore the frissons of excitement running down her arm.

As she stood up, Vittorio drew her against him. 'It's been a wonderful evening, Lucy. Just having you with me…'

He broke off as once more he felt his treacherous body leading him on to prolong the encounter. He had to cool it. He had to distance himself from Lucy before she bewitched him again.

'We've both got emotional problems, haven't we?' he said quietly. 'Neither of us wants to become committed or too involved. We're both still trying to get over our previous relationships. Yours was a relationship you're trying to forget. Mine was a relationship I was clinging to…until tonight.'

'Tonight?' Her heart was thudding.

Vittorio knew he should stay silent but he couldn't. 'Didn't you feel it, Lucy?' he said, his voice alive with passion. 'When we sat by the Trevi fountains? All around us were young, romantic couples…'

He broke off, knowing that he mustn't elaborate on his feelings. He mustn't disclose how he'd been tempted to think that love, real love just might be possible again…with the right woman…with someone like Lucy.

No, he mustn't think like that ever again. Just because he could feel himself coming alive again, it wasn't worth taking the risk. If he allowed himself to fall in love with Lucy, even to imagine that he was being given a second chance, he would be at the mercy of his emotions for the whole of their relationship.

He bent his head and kissed her gently on the lips.

One kiss, one innocent little goodnight kiss was all he would allow himself...

But Lucy turned her head upwards, savouring the feel of Vittorio's kiss. Vittorio gave a deep sigh as he recognised that he couldn't fight against Lucy's deep emotional magnetism. He was only made of flesh and blood, for heaven's sake! He'd tried to resist the temptation but the touch of her lips was undermining all his resolutions.

Lucy sighed as she revelled in the feeling of Vittorio's hands caressing her so slowly, so tantalisingly slowly. She could feel her body reacting with a longing she hadn't felt before. Here was a man who was making her feel like a real woman again. But the little voice in her head was saying, Can you trust him? Won't he let you down as Mark did? Does he tell lies? Will he break your heart?

She was arching her back so that she could mould herself against him. At some point in her life she would have to start trusting again. Perhaps it was time she took a chance? And with the strong erotic feelings she was experiencing she wanted more than anything to trust Vittorio. And she wanted to trust him soon...maybe tonight... She wanted him to take her to his bed and...

His caressing hands were driving her wild. His tantalising fingers were exploring her body while his kisses were almost too much to bear. Deep down inside her, every fibre of her being was crying out for consummation. It would be so easy to lose herself now...so easy... But the black doubts were still there. Just supposing...

'No!' She pulled herself away. 'I'm sorry, Vittorio. I shouldn't have led you on like that. I...I'm not ready. I need time...'

Vittorio was trying to steady his breathing. He was panting as if he'd been running in a race. It was difficult to come down to earth again when he'd been so utterly consumed by his attraction to Lucy. Another moment and he would have carried her off to his bedroom and made love to her, so slowly, so gently, so ultimately satisfyingly.

If he'd kept to the resolutions he'd made this evening he would have already taken Lucy back to her room before they'd been able reignite the dormant passion that sprang so easily between them. They were both vulnerable people who knew they mustn't jump into a heavy relationship ever again.

'Of course you need time,' he said huskily as he tried to regain his composure.

Whatever happened between Lucy and himself, he must always put her needs first. He must never do anything to hurt her.

'We both need time,' he went on, leaning back against the cushions, one arm casually laid across the back of the sofa. 'Exploring a new relationship isn't easy when we've both suffered. But it's exciting to meet someone who understands, isn't it?'

Oh, yes, it was exciting. Exciting and confusing! Lucy had no idea what the future held but she hoped that perhaps she and Vittorio would be able to have a light, no-strings-attached romance. She looked up into Vittorio's eyes, relief flooding through her as she realised that he really understood the situation in the same way that she did.

'That's exactly how I feel.'

Vittorio took her hand. 'Come on, I'll take you to your room.'

She laced her fingers through his as they walked down the corridor. At her door, he reached down and kissed her gently on the lips. Then he turned and walked quickly away. She put her key in the door. Her hands were shaking. She was still undecided about whether she'd done the right thing by calling a halt at that crucial point of no return. In her heart she knew she wanted to call out and ask Vittorio to take her back to his room. But the moment had gone.

As she pushed open the door she tried to convince herself that it made sense to ease herself slowly into this relationship. She wasn't yet ready for any kind of commitment. And neither was Vittorio.

She lay down on her bed, staring up at the ceiling as she thought about the future. Neither she nor Vittorio would want commitment to a relationship in the future. Vittorio had made it perfectly clear that he would never dare to love again. He was so obviously frightened of having his heart broken again if he were to lose the love of his life.

And she, in a different way, felt exactly the same. Mark had been a swine but, yes, she had loved the man she'd thought he'd been. And to love again would bring with it the kind of commitment she wasn't prepared to take. So a light-hearted romance with Vittorio was all she was looking for...wasn't it?

Yes, she told herself firmly. Marriage, babies, permanent relationships were out. They happened to other people...but not to her.

As she thought about babies, she groaned, putting her hand on her abdomen, over the empty uterus where her baby had been. She remembered the pain of the miscarriage. The terrible realisation that she was losing her baby. That its life was draining away from her. And then, after she'd been taken to hospital, the pain of the D and C when the surgeon had made sure they'd taken away all remnants of her child.

Her gynaecological consultant had advised her to return to check that the operation hadn't caused any complications that might affect her chance of becoming pregnant in the future. But she'd been tramatised, desperately trying to forget her disastrous relationship with Mark. The last thing she'd wanted was to think about a future pregnancy. That would have involved a relationship with a man, and that was something she'd been planning to avoid.

Until she'd met Vittorio. Even now, she was trying her hardest to resist the temptation of wishing for the moon. Wishing that she could trust Vittorio. Hoping that he was a trustworthy man who wanted her as much as…

She checked her stupid romantic notions as they threatened to take over her rational self. She mustn't start looking too far ahead. It was enough for the moment that she was beginning to trust again. Next time…if there was a next time!

Everything had happened so quickly! It had only been a week since she'd met Vittorio. That was why she didn't want to rush into something she might regret.

She turned over and buried her head in her pillow. Life was so complicated! If you'd been hurt badly it was so difficult to view becoming involved in a relationship.

She jumped up from her bed and went into her tiny shower room. Standing under the shower, soaping herself, feeling the warm suds flowing over her aching body, she felt calmer. She stepped out of the shower and wrapped herself in a large fluffy towel.

If there was a next time when she and Vittorio were alone, she would relax more and go with the flow. Mmm…the thought of Vittorio's strong arms wrapped around her was sending shivers of excitement down her spine…

Vittorio was lying in the bath, staring up at the steamy tiles, watching a spider on the ceiling trying to make itself invisible because it knew that Vittorio was watching it.

'It's OK,' Vittorio told the spider. 'I don't kill spiders. Anyway, it would be too much trouble to climb up there tonight. I'm actually very tired.'

Tired and a little dispirited, he thought as he sank back into the foamy suds. He'd poured nearly half a bottle of the scented stuff one of his sisters had given him for his last birthday. It occurred to him now that if ever he gave in to the desire to persuade Lucy to stay the night with him, he could empty in the other half and they could bathe together before…and after…and…

He groaned. If he'd taken Lucy to bed tonight, it could have been the first time she'd tried to trust a man since her odious boyfriend had betrayed her. Was Lucy so scarred by the experience of utter betrayal that she would never be able to trust again?

He hoped not. He gave a deep sigh and lifted up the glass of champagne he'd placed at the side of the bath, taking a deep gulp. Because if he was careful, very very careful, he might be able to enjoy a light-hearted relationship with Lucy that they would both enjoy. A non-committed, no-strings-on-either-side relationship where he would try his hardest not to fall in love…if that were possible with someone as wonderfully beautiful and charismatic as Lucy.

Throughout the next week, Lucy had the distinct feeling that Vittorio was holding something back from her. Whenever they had to work together he was his usual charming self but he didn't make any attempt to suggest they meet in the evening.

She'd come to the conclusion that she'd put him off by making it clear she'd wanted to go back to her room when she could have stayed longer...much longer! Another week on, she found herself watching Vittorio's expression as he sutured the end of a little boy's finger. He was concentrating one hundred per cent, looking very serious and single-minded.

She realised that over the two weeks she'd known Vittorio she'd come to appreciate all his moods, serious, frivolous, romantic...especially romantic! She felt the familiar longing deep down inside to spend more time with him. Would there be any chance that this might happen tonight? Maybe?

But for the rest of the day they had to stay focused on their patients. This little patient was a seven-year-old English boy who was staying with his Italian grandmother for the summer. The grandmother had been beside herself when she'd brought Darren in. She'd heavily bandaged the end of the finger which had been almost severed by the scissors he'd found in his grandmother's sewing basket.

'Can I go now?' Darren asked Lucy, pleading with his eyes, red-rimmed from crying.

Lucy held the little boy more tightly against her. 'Not yet, darling. Vittorio hasn't quite finished. Just another few minutes.'

Lucy had decided against sending the boy to Theatre. The tip of the finger was held firmly in place by a small section of skin and underlying tissue. She'd known that the quicker she could secure the tip back on the finger, the more chance there was that the nerves and blood supply could be connected again. All the theatres were full at the moment, so she'd asked Vittorio, in his ca-

pacity as acting director, if she could go ahead in trying
to reconnect the tip of the finger.

Vittorio had said it was a good idea but he would
prefer to do the reconnection himself. It wasn't that he
doubted Lucy's expertise but he'd recently had a case
which had gone to Theatre and hadn't been successful.
Vittorio believed that too much time had unavoidably
passed between the time of the accident and the time of
the surgery. He wanted to prove to himself that emergency surgery under a local anaesthetic in Pronto
Soccorso could be a viable proposition.

So Lucy had administered the local anaesthetic and
then sat down holding the little boy on her lap while
Vittorio performed the delicate operation.

Darren's grandmother was sitting outside the cubicle,
waiting anxiously to hear if her grandson would have a
complete finger. She'd said she didn't want to watch and
she knew that Darren was in safe hands.

'Vittorio has nearly finished now, Darren,' Lucy said.

'Where's Nonna?'

'She's sitting outside.'

'Will she buy me an ice cream when we go home?'

'I expect she will when it's time for you to go home.'

Lucy looked up at Vittorio, her eyes questioning him
to see if she should divulge the news that Darren would
have to spend the night in hospital. Vittorio glanced up
at Lucy and nodded in agreement.

'You're going to sleep here in the hospital tonight,
Darren. There'll be some other boys and girls in beds
nearby you so you'll be able to talk to them. And there
are toys in the children's ward.'

'Have you got many toys in there?' Darren asked solemnly.

'Oh, yes! We've got lots of toys in the children's ward. There's a big playroom beside the ward.'

'OK, I'll stay. Why can't I feel my finger any more, Lucy?'

'You'll soon feel it again. I made it numb when I pricked that local anaesthetic in.'

'Local anaesthetic,' Darren repeated carefully. 'Wait till I tell Nonna what's in there. She speaks a bit of English, but not much.'

'But you speak Italian, don't you, Darren?'

'Of course. My mum spoke Italian all the time before I went to school. My dad speaks English when he's at home, which isn't often because he drives a big truck and he's always going off somewhere. So I found it a bit hard to talk to my friends when I first went to school. I'm OK now, though.'

'All finished, Darren,' Vittorio announced as he snipped at the last suture. 'Now, you mustn't get this wet. And you mustn't be rough with this hand. Try to do everything with your other hand for a few days, will you?'

'OK. Do you have ice cream in this hospital?'

'Of course!' Lucy said, setting the little boy down on his feet.

'Tutti-frutti?' Darren persisted. 'That's the one with the fruit and all the different flavours. You can't get that in England, well, not round where we live.'

'Let's go and see what we can find,' Lucy said, taking holding of Darren's good hand. 'But first we need to talk to Nonna and tell her what's happening.'

After settling Darren in the children's ward with his ice cream, Lucy hurried back to Pronto Soccorso. The department had been relatively quiet all day which was why two doctors had been able to take care of one small boy. But towards the end of the peaceful afternoon there was a car crash close by on the road by the river. One car had braked too quickly, another had run into the back of it, followed by the knock-on effect of a pile-up involving several cars.

Lucy and Vittorio, along with all available staff pulled in from other areas of the hospital, were kept busy even after the night staff arrived. Lucy was particularly concerned about a late arrival from the crash. A large woman, who now lay in front of her on the stretcher, was moaning softly. Until minutes ago she'd been trapped in the wreckage of her car. She'd been unconscious for most of the time but was just coming round and pain was obviously kicking in.

'I'm Dottore Lucy. Can you hear me?'

The woman nodded. 'Am I in hospital?' she asked in the fascinating accent of someone from southern Italy.

'Yes, you are.'

There were no case notes with Lucy's patient. The paramedics said she'd been unconscious and so they hadn't been able to talk to her as they'd struggled to extricate her from the wreckage of her car. It was up to Lucy to make a quick assessment of her condition.

She decided to put in a line to rehydrate her. Then she pulled back the sheet that covered her patient up to her chin to make a preliminary examination and check what injuries she'd sustained. Looking down at the woman's abdomen, she immediately noticed that beneath the layer of clothing there was a definite swelling. The woman was obese but her condition was obviously more than too much fatty tissue.

'*Come si chiama?* What's your name?' Lucy asked.

'*Io sono* Katarina. I think I need to go to the toilet. I

have a big pain coming in my bottom. I need to go quickly.'

Lucy placed her hands on her patient's abdomen. 'When is your baby due, Katarina?'

'Baby? I have no baby.'

Lucy could feel the uterus contracting beneath her fingers. The contractions were coming quickly.

'Aagh!' Katarina groaned, and began clutching the sides of the trolley.

Vittorio came in from the next cubicle and looked enquiringly at Lucy.

'My patient's in labour,' she told him in Italian, wanting to make sure that her patient knew what was going on and would co-operate with them.

'Yes, yes, I am going to have a baby,' Katarina said. 'I tried to tell myself there is no baby. But's too soon. I'm not ready for a baby. I have to—aagh!'

Lucy reached for the enotonox machine and slipped the mask over her patient's face. 'Take deep breaths, Katarina. This will ease the pain.'

Vittorio had quickly scrubbed up at the sink and was investigating the size of the birth canal.

'The cervix is fully dilated, Lucy. The baby's head is visible. Show Katarina how to pant. She mustn't push yet. Hold back! The head is being born now… Hold still, Katarina. Let me check on the umbilical cord.'

At the top end of the examination couch, Lucy was helping to soothe her patient and directing when she could push and when she should pant. As Vittorio gave her the signal that her patient could push on the next contraction, she wiped Katarina's forehead with some cooling water.

'Nearly there, Katarina. Baby's almost… Yes, you can push now.'

'I'm holding the head and the body.' Vittorio spoke quietly but his excitement was obvious.

'The baby's legs are almost here,' Vittorio continued after a few moments almost under his breath.

He raised his voice. 'You've got a little girl, Katarina.'

Their patient gave a huge grin. *'Grazie, grazie, Dottore!'*

'Is your husband with you?' Lucy asked gently as she watched Vittorio cutting the cord.

'I have no husband. He left me for another woman. But I have a new boyfriend. He made me pregnant. I don't know if he likes children so I didn't tell him about my baby.'

Lucy took the slippery baby in her arms, gently swabbing her eyes and making sure that she could breathe easily through her nostrils and mouth. She was a big, beautiful, perfectly formed baby, definitely full term. Her little dimpled hands were curling and uncurling as she gave loud lusty cries of protest as Lucy checked her over.

'You didn't want to come out of your cosy nest, did you, my precious?' Lucy whispered as she wrapped the baby in a dressing towel and gave her to Katarina.

'Ah, magnifico! Bella, bella, bellissima…'

Lucy swallowed hard. The feel of the baby in her arms had been so comforting to her senses. Whenever she worked on delivering a baby nowadays she had to steel herself against the strong rush of maternal instincts when the baby was born. Seeing the mother holding the baby now, knowing that her patient had succeeded where she'd failed, brought back all the awful memories of her miscarriage.

She took a deep breath. She had to remain professional, had to stay calm for the sake of her patient and her baby. Personal emotions were of no use when you were a doctor.

She glanced up and saw that Vittorio was watching her, a concerned expression on his face. Was she giving too much away? She didn't want to tell Vittorio the second part of the story about her life-changing relationship with Mark. Well, not yet, anyway. Maybe one day...

She moved back to the examination couch so that she could give all her attention to her patient.

Tears were rolling down the new mother's cheeks as she cuddled her baby.

'Would you like me to call your boyfriend, Katarina?' Vittorio asked. 'I'm sure when he sees your beautiful little daughter he will be so happy.'

Katarina looked over the baby's head at the handsome doctor. 'You think so?'

'This is your boyfriend's child as well as yours. Of course he'll love her! You are a real family now. Give me the number and I'll...'

Katarina rattled off a number and Vittorio wrote it down.

'Now, you're going to be taken to Obstetrics,' Lucy said. 'The doctor and nurses there will carry out a number of checks to make sure that all is well with you and the baby.'

A midwife appeared with a porter. 'Do you have a patient for Obstetrics in here, Lucy?'

'We certainly have. Katarina and her baby will require full postnatal checks and a bed in the obstetrics ward.'

The midwife smiled down at the new mother who was cradling her baby against her.

'So you didn't want to have your baby in our department, then, Katarina?'

'I wanted the handsome doctor to deliver my baby,' Katarina said, as she was wheeled away.

Lucy smiled up at Vittorio. 'And how is the handsome doctor feeling at the end of this long day?'

Vittorio grinned. 'If you're referring to me,' he said in English, 'I'm feeling as if I need some fresh air, followed by a cold bottle of wine shared with a beautiful woman.'

'Ah, but where will you find a beautiful woman at short notice?'

'Problems, problems! I could make do with…'

Vittorio put his finger under Lucy's chin and lifted it up so that she had to look him full in the face. 'I could make do with someone who had long blonde hair, fabulous blue eyes, perfect features, a luscious extremely kissable mouth…yes, I think that adds up to a beautiful woman, don't you?'

He bent his head and kissed her gently on the lips. They were alone in the cubicle but that didn't mean that somebody wouldn't walk in at any moment. Lucy savoured the touch of his mouth on hers, feeling her treacherous body reacting to the nearness of the virile, charismatic man she was falling hopelessly in love with. In spite of everything she'd told herself about never trusting again, she was finding herself in the same position she'd been before she'd given herself to Mark.

'Are you free tonight?' Vittorio whispered as he pulled away, his hands still holding her firmly by the shoulders as he looked down at her with a devastatingly tender expression.

She could feel herself going weak at the knees. Was she free? She would have cancelled any engagement to spend more time with Vittorio!

'I think I might be,' she said softly. 'What did you have in mind?'

'I just happen to have tickets for the opera. It's a special performance for charity. I bought the tickets ages ago not knowing whether or not I would be able to go. Will you come with me?'

'Which opera is it tonight?' Lucy asked.

It sounded as if her answer depended on what was being performed that evening, but Lucy knew she would have sat in a theatre and stared at an empty stage all evening if that was what Vittorio had in mind!

'It's *La Boheme*.'

'Oh, how wonderful!' She couldn't disguise her enthusiasm. 'My favourite opera. We'll hear the duet between Mimi and Rudolpho when they meet for the first time. When I dipped my hand in the Trevi fountain two weeks ago, you were singing Rudolpho's part as you wiped my hand and…'

She broke off, realising that the emotion in her voice was blatant. She was giving herself away. Showing how moved she'd been when Vittorio had sung to her.

He drew her against him. 'So you will come with me tonight?'

'I'd love to.'

'We'll sit outside on the terrace at Giovanni's and have a drink first. It's such a beautiful evening. The opera is going to be held at the Colosseum. It's a special outdoor performance.'

'But do we have time for a drink first? Won't we be late?'

Vittorio smiled down at her. 'This is Rome, Lucy. Rome in the middle of summer. People have the time to take a siesta in the afternoons during our long hot summer. Then they come out at night and stay out enjoying themselves until dawn. The performance starts late and finishes after midnight. We'll be able to have a late supper somewhere.'

'After midnight?' Lucy said. 'Don't you mean breakfast?'

She held her breath as she realised what she'd said.

'If you like, you can have breakfast,' Vittorio said softly, as he nuzzled his face against her hair. 'I'm sure that can be arranged...'

The cubicle door was opening. Lucy pulled herself away and put on a serious expression.

'*Mi scusi, Dottore Vittorio,*' a young night nurse said. 'Shall I come back later?'

'No, we're just going.'

Vittorio put out his arm to detain Lucy as they stepped outside. 'Can you meet me in ten minutes?'

'You must be joking! I have to shower, change, decide what to wear...'

'Lucy, this isn't London. We're going to an outdoor performance. Keep it casual. Don't dress up, dress down.'

'Half an hour,' Lucy said, moving swiftly away.

'Maximum!' Vittorio called after her.

CHAPTER FOUR

BACK in her room, Lucy surveyed her wardrobe. Vittorio had said she should dress down but she didn't want to take any chances. All those chic Italian women who'd had the time for a siesta during the long hot afternoon wouldn't be dressing down! They'd know exactly what they were going to wear and they would have probably had their garments laid out ready to wear all afternoon.

She didn't have many clothes with her. She didn't have many clothes, full stop. Her hand lingered over the pink floaty thing she'd bought on impulse during a rare day out in Leeds earlier that year.

As she dashed into the shower and turned on the water she was remembering that day vividly. It had been a turning point for her. For months she'd been unable to shake off the sadness of losing her baby. If she'd known the agony she would have to go through, she'd never have agreed to get pregnant in the first place. Innate maternal love was the strongest emotion she'd ever felt.

It had been Mark's idea that they should try for a baby. She'd resisted at first, saying that she loved her work at the hospital. She didn't think she was ready to be a mother especially when she saw the father so infrequently.

But Mark had been adamant that he wanted them to be a family. He'd been such a charismatic, persuasive character. He'd told her he was due to stop flying soon and take an important job in London. They would get married, live in a lovely house…

As she stepped out of the shower she wondered why she hadn't seen through all that. But on the day that Mark had broken down and wept because she'd found him out, he'd explained that being with her in the cottage had been his escape from reality. Reality had been his dull wife, two demanding children and a huge mortgage. But when he'd been with Lucy he'd deluded himself into thinking that he could make his dreams come true.

As he'd talked to her she'd come to the conclusion that he needed to see a psychiatrist. But she'd decided it hadn't been her place to tell him. She'd been angry with him, yes, but she'd simply wanted him to get out of her life. She hadn't even told him she was two months pregnant. Not after he'd told her what a pain his children were and how furious he'd been that his wife had got herself pregnant again when she'd supposedly been on the Pill!

She sat there listening to his tirade about his awful domestic circumstances and realised that she loved her unborn baby too much to allow Mark to share in her pregnancy. After the baby was born she would contact him, tell him she'd had his child, make sure he understood that he could see the child, acknowledge it as his own if he so wished. But she wanted as little contact with him as possible. But for the sake of the child he could have as much or as little access as he wanted.

And for a further month she was able to continue cherishing her unborn child. Until that awful morning, in the middle of transfering a patient to Theatre, she felt as if someone had stuck a knife in her back. She doubled over, feeling the warm, horrible sticky blood draining out of her…

That was in the autumn and her physical and emotional wounds were still hurting on that day in Leeds when she simply wanted to forget and try to pull herself together again. She continued to work full time after the miscarriage, which helped to blot out some of the emotional pain, but what she didn't do was use her off-duty days in completely frivolous pursuits.

She saw the floaty, chiffon frock in the window of a little dress shop just off Bond Street. The saleswoman had just finished fixing it on the model and Lucy stopped to admire it. The saleswoman smiled at her and Lucy decided to go in and take a further look. There might be an occasion when she needed a frock like that…

Half an hour later she emerged sporting a carrier bag with the designer logo emblazoned on the outside. For a few minutes she felt thrilled with her purchase, but as she drove back to her cottage in the Dales she decided she must have had a moment of madness. When on earth would she ever wear something so divinely useless? Perhaps she would simply drift around the house in it occasionally, pretending she was a lady of leisure or something.

But it made her feel good about herself again. She was confident she would soon be back to normal. As if on cue, Sarah phoned that evening to say she was pregnant and would be taking three months' maternity leave. And Lucy knew exactly what she should do. She should ask if she could take over Sarah's job for three months.

Back in the present, standing in her bra and pants, she carefully, almost reverently took the dress from its hanger. Yes, tonight was the night when she would give her dress its premiere! She would have not only a moment of madness but a whole evening! And if breakfast was on offer afterwards, after the performance…or whatever, especially whatever, that would be perfect.

'I hardly recognised you when you came into Reception tonight,' Vittorio said as he raised his wineglass towards Lucy.

Lucy looked out across the terrace at Enotecca Giovani and smiled. She'd enjoyed the look of admiration in Vittorio's eyes as she'd emerged.

'You mean I usually look different?'

Vittorio leaned forward to take her hand. 'You always look beautiful to me, even in the white coat that hides your lovely figure.'

Lucy could feel her heart thumping madly. It was going to be a good evening. Vittorio raised his glass towards her.

Vittorio knew he was playing a dangerous game. Shouldn't he try to be less effusive? Wouldn't his admiration be misinterpreted? But was it possible to feel as he did and remain cool?

As they clinked glasses she could feel the excitement rising inside her. If buying the dress had been a turning point, actually wearing it was adding to her confidence. Yes, she really was back on form, back to the old Lucy...or was it the new Lucy? The dress had helped but, more than anything else, admitting to herself that she was falling in love with Vittorio and allowing it to happen was even more life-changing. But dare she risk going along with the exciting feelings that were surging through her? Was Vittorio really someone she could trust? She'd known him such a short time.

Vittorio had arranged for a taxi to pick them up from Giovanni's. They sat close together in the back, Vittorio's arm resting casually on the back of the seat. Lucy glanced sideways so she could admire the suave, confident, sexy man beside her. The glass of wine she'd drunk at Giovanni's seemed to have gone to her head. As she looked at Vittorio she felt a surge of sensual longing for him.

He turned to look at her and she blushed. It was a good thing he couldn't read her thoughts! Much as she was looking forward to the opera tonight, she was even more excited about the prospect of being alone with Vittorio afterwards.

As they took their seats in the ancient amphitheatre of the Colosseum Lucy was glad she'd dressed up rather than down. This was a charity event and the tickets were expensive so a lot of important people had turned out to show their support. There were a few ladies in evening gowns, carrying cashmere stoles or pashminas to wear as the evening cooled down towards midnight. Many people were wearing what could only be described as smart casual but Lucy deduced that it was a well-heeled audience.

'I believe I told you this was a one-off performance,' Vittorio said as she studied the programme. 'The Colosseum has had to be specially prepared for tonight's performance. The tiers of seats have had to be strengthened in some places.'

'I like the small cushions that have been provided. *La Boheme* is a long opera. It will be after midnight before we leave.'

Vittorio smiled. 'If you fall asleep, I shall simply lay you across my lap and hold you safely until it's time to go.'

Lucy smiled back. She'd heard that Italian men were romantic. But she was sure that tonight she was out with the most romantic man in the whole of Rome! She smoothed down her flowing chiffon skirt, glad that she'd spent a few moments rubbing hand cream into her skin.

Having to scrub up several times a day made her hands rough so she pampered them whenever possible.

Vittorio reached across and touched the flimsy fabric. 'So delicate, so absolutely you.'

'You think so? I wasn't sure when I bought it. It's not the kind of dress I usually wear. My clothes are usually completely practical.'

'Practical clothes for practical situations, but tonight you look like a princess so that is how I shall treat you,' Vittorio said, his dark, charismatic eyes tender with admiration, his voice husky.

Lucy felt a shiver of excitement as she looked up into his eyes. Stifling a sigh of longing for what was to come later, she looked down at the area where the performance was to take place. A stage had been erected in the middle of the arena. The orchestra had assembled and had finished tuning up. An expectant hush fell on the audience.

There were a few moments of absolute silence and then the musicians began to play the overture with its hauntingly moving, well-known, agelessly popular themes that gave a taste of what was to follow. The music captured exactly the excitement of the happiness of the two lovers at the beginning of their romance, followed by impending anguish that arrived at the end of the story.

The overture finished and immediately the first act began. The singing was superb. Lucy found herself tremendously moved by the music in the first part of the opera. And her attention was held throughout the following scenes.

Lucy was aware that Vittorio was sitting closely beside her. At one moment of pathos during the opera, he took hold of her hand, gently caressing her fingers. She turned to look at him in the dim light cast from the stage and the already bright light of the moon. Their eyes met and Vittorio smiled, a knowing smile. A promise of what was to come later when they were alone perhaps?

'I love the first part of *La Boheme*,' she said to Vittorio as they settled down for the final act, 'but because I've seen the opera a few times and I know the anguish that Rudolpho and Mimi will have to go through, I feel terribly apprehensive towards the end. I almost wish I could rewrite the script, so that they could have a happy ending.'

Vittorio reached for her hand again. 'I know exactly what you mean. But the opera is mirroring real life, isn't it? Life doesn't always turn out how you want it to and you don't get a second chance. However you plan things, you...'

He broke off, swallowing hard. Glancing sideways, Lucy could see the moistness in his eyes. He was reliving the tragedy in his life. Why did she always get the feeling that Vittorio was withholding some dark secret? She lifted his hand to her lips and gently kissed his long, sensitive fingers. He leaned forward and brushed his lips across her cheek.

'Thank you,' he whispered. 'Thank you for understanding. I'll never be able to forget but I'm sure I can get on with my life...now that...'

Lucy waited but Vittorio's voice had choked again. She hoped he'd been going to say he could go forward now that she was with him. Perhaps in time he would be able to do that.

As the opera drew to a close and Rudolpho's anguish as Mimi lay dying became more and more poignant, Lucy found herself clinging to Vittorio's hand. He was the strong one now. He seemed to have steeled himself for the intense sadness of Rudolpho's loss.

As the rapturous audience clapped and cheered the soloists and cast at the end of the performance, Vittorio smiled at Lucy.

She smiled back. 'Rudolpho and Mimi are fully recovered now. I'm always glad to see them come back on stage after all that suffering.'

'If only life was that easy,' Vittorio said, his voice rich in emotion.

'But we're all the stronger when we come through the bad times,' Lucy said. 'In England we have a saying that when one door shuts another opens. Have you ever heard that?'

'I have now,' Vittorio said, putting his arm around her shoulders as he guided her to the exit.

They were being swallowed up by the crowd as they reached the kerbside, attempting to hail a taxi.

'Let's walk,' Lucy suggested.

'We'll head for the river,' Vittorio said, shielding her from a large man who had planted himself firmly in the middle of the crowd.

They walked along beside the swirling Tiber. The moon was shining on the water, giving it an iridescent sheen. Lucy didn't feel the least bit tired even though it was way past midnight.

'We'll stop at the first restaurant or bar that's still open and have some supper,' Vittorio said. 'Are you hungry?'

'Not really,' she said.

He stopped and drew her against him. 'So, would you settle for an early breakfast?'

In the moonlight she could see the tender expression on his face and a frisson of excitement ran down her spine.

'I'd like that,' she said softly.

Vittorio bent his head and kissed her.

It took only minutes to walk back to the hospital and reach Vittorio's room. As he put his key in the lock, Lucy felt a frisson of excitement mixed with apprehension. This would be a big step for both of them if they made love tonight.

She looked up at Vittorio as he closed the door and drew her against him. For a few moments she felt impossibly shy. Vittorio must realise that this time she really was longing to stay the night with him. The expression in his eyes was tender, hauntingly tender as he bent his head to kiss her. She parted her lips, savouring the touch of his mouth against hers, the delicate, intimate movement of his tongue.

His hands were caressing her back, his fingers were stimulating every sensory nerve so that she felt as if an electric current was running down her spine.

He broke away to pull off his jacket, tossing it impatiently towards the sofa before reaching for her again. His hands were caressing her through the flimsy dress until he found the buttons he was searching for and began deftly to unhook them. Feverishly, Lucy undid Vittorio's shirt. As he pulled it over his head she felt her excitement mounting. The muscles on his chest were firm, rippling beneath the tanned, sun-kissed skin.

In a matter of moments their clothes were strewn on the floor and skin pressed against skin. Vittorio lifted her and carried her through to the bedroom. The sheet was already turned back. Vittorio laid her down gently, tenderly, whispering to her all the time in Italian, the beautiful language whose musical tones seemed made for romance.

Some of the phrases she hadn't heard before, but she

knew instinctively what Vittorio meant. He was saying how wonderful he thought she was, how he loved being with her. She hoped this was true, that it wasn't just in the heat of a passionate moment that he felt like this towards her...

She lay back against her pillows, looking up at the ornate ceiling. How very Italian this room was. So very artistic. Where would you find a beautiful ceiling like that in the residents' quarters of an English hospital?

Vittorio was still asleep. After they'd made love, she'd slept in Vittorio's arms, feeling ecstatically happy. She remembered now how she'd felt at the moment of climax. It had been like drowning in a sea of sensual wonder, and as she'd come up for air from the depths of this sea she'd felt as if she'd floated up to heaven, weightless, ethereal, her whole body tingling with divine sensation.

She drew in her breath as she realised she was still tingling. Her body would never be the same again now that she'd experienced that ecstatic consummation with Vittorio. She looked across the pillows and gently stroked his dark, tousled hair.

He opened his eyes and gave her a languid smile as he reached out for her and drew her against him.

'Cara mia, mio tesoro.' His lips brushed her cheek, lightly caressing her skin with his tongue. 'Mmm, you taste so good. I want to eat all of you. I want to consume every little part of you...'

Their naked bodies were entwined again. She could feel Vittorio's hard virile manhood pressing against her and her own body seemed to turn into liquid fire once more. She'd thought she'd been satiated when she'd fallen asleep but every part of her was tuning into Vittorio's erotic caresses.

This time their love-making was unhurried, each of them trying to make the divine experience last as long as possible. But Vittorio's caresses were driving her wild with a seemingly insatiable desire.

'Yes, oh, yes,' she whispered as Vittorio led her towards the magic of their consummation. As she felt him moving inside her, rhythmically, relentlessly, teasingly, sending her nearer and nearer to the ecstasy she knew was awaiting her, she felt she couldn't wait for the final moments any longer.

She cried out as wave after wave of climactic excitement tore through her entire body, clinging to Vittorio as if she would never let him go, holding him inside her as if he belonged there…

When she opened her eyes again, after falling into a deep dreamless sleep, the sun was peeping over the window-sill. Still low in the sky, but it was time they should start to be waking up. Lucy swung her legs over the side of the bed, only to find that her movements had awakened Vittorio and he was reaching out towards her, trying to entice her back to bed.

She laughingly tried to protest as he teased the back of her neck with his tongue. 'Vittorio, we need to start moving…'

'I am moving! Can't you feel that I'm—?'

'Vittorio, we do have to go on duty this morning and—'

'OK, you win, but I'll beat you to the bathroom!'

They raced across the polished wooden floors like a couple of children competing at school sports day. Vittorio caught her in his arms as they reached the bathroom door.

'It's a large bath,' he said as he bent down to snuggle his head against her hair. 'Room for both of us so we don't need to compete for who's first in there.'

He raised his head. 'With or without?'

She smiled. 'What are we talking about now?'

'Bath foam, of course! Do you want me to soap you all over or would you prefer to soak for a while?'

'Both!'

'I'm sure that can be arranged.'

Vittorio began pouring different lotions into the bath before putting his hands underneath her and sweeping her over the side of the bath, gently lowering her into the fragrant foam.

Like a couple of lovesick teenagers they played with the foam, flicking it against each other, before the mood changed and they curled around each other, spoon-shaped. Vittorio leaned against the back of the bath, Lucy pressed herself against him, feeling that she'd never been in such a blissful situation and wondering how long this feeling of happiness could last once she got out into the real world again.

'This is the long soak you asked for,' Vittorio whispered as his hands caressed her breasts, his fingers tantalisingly arousing her senses again. 'But it comes at a price…'

She turned to face him, looking up into his dark eyes. 'How much?'

'For you, *senorita*, one kiss.' Vittorio bent his head and kissed her slowly and tenderly, his tongue tantalising her once more until she could feel her body rousing to meet the blatantly obvious need that she could feel in Vittorio…

*   *   *

'I feel like a dolphin,' Lucy said, as she lay back in the foamy water, once more in a spoon-shaped embrace with Vittorio.

'How do you know that's how dolphins make love?' Vittorio asked her teasingly.

'I merely meant that all that splashing around in the water was...' She broke off as she looked over the side of the bath. 'Talking of all that splashing around in the water, have you seen the state of your bathroom carpet, Vittorio?'

'Oh, it will dry! It's not important. Let's—'

'No, let's climb out. Hours ago, you promised me breakfast, remember?'

'I'm absolutely starving!' Lucy said as she began to eat her share of the huge breakfast omelette Vittorio had prepared.

They were sitting in the small kitchen, Lucy in one of Vittorio's robes which was much too big for her. Underneath she was wearing nothing but the bare skin that Vittorio had pampered and caressed in the bath they'd shared. Her hair, still damp from their long playful soak followed by their even longer love-making in the foamy bath, was spread out over the collar of Vittorio's robe.

Vittorio looked across the table and smiled. 'You look very young without make-up. I think you should go into Pronto Soccorso looking exactly like that this morning.'

'Your robe's a bit too big for me,' Lucy said, as she swallowed some more omelette before taking a sip of her coffee.

Vittorio grinned. 'I'll turn the sleeves up for you.'

Lucy laughed. 'OK. I'll go like this if you'll go like that.'

She pointed at his bare muscular chest. His only garment was a towel wrapped around his waist.

'Why not?' Vittorio stretched his hand across the table and caressed Lucy's fingers. 'I feel as if I could do anything today. How about you?'

She nodded. 'This is one day when I really would like to do nothing.'

'Nothing?' Vittorio raised an eyebrow.

Lucy smiled. 'Well, you know what I mean.'

Vittorio stood up and came round the table to put an arm around her shoulder.

'I hope I do know what you mean. Because it's not time to go to the hospital yet. We've got almost half an hour before we need to.'

'Vittorio, I meant…'

But Vittorio's hands were tantalisingly tempting her again. She abandoned her half-eaten omelette and stood up so that she could press herself against him. With one swift movement of his hand he undid the loose tie of her robe. Their skins touched again and Lucy gave a sigh of renewed excitement as Vittorio swept her up into his arms.

It was very strange that morning in Pronto Soccorso as Lucy tried to come down to earth. Listening to Vittorio now as he chaired one of the regular meetings between the medical staff of Pronto Soccorso and the staff who'd cared for the patients they'd admitted during their follow-up treatment, Lucy found it hard to believe that only a short time ago she'd been making wild, exciting love with this distinguished, charismatic and totally professional doctor.

Vittorio was looking suave, cool, fully in control and capable of answering any question that he was asked. Looking at him, Lucy knew that no one would have the slightest notion of how he'd spent the night! He seemed as if he'd had his full quota of sleep and was perfectly rested, whereas…

She gave herself a quick reprimand as she forced herself to concentrate on what was being said at the meeting. They were beginning the review of patients who'd been treated during the last couple of weeks. The minor injuries were quickly dispensed with. No problems had presented themselves. There was no patient in that category who could have received any better treatment.

'The object of these regular reviews between all the staff who liaise with Pronto Soccorso,' Vittorio was saying in rapid but clearly enunciated Italian, 'is to see how we can improve our services, how we can make things better for the patient and more efficient for the medical staff.'

There was a murmur of agreement. For a moment, Lucy's eyes met Vittorio's. For an instant, his cool, professional expression softened, his eyes held that tender look that sent shivers down her spine.

But the moment had already passed. Vittorio was making a deliberate effort to focus on the task in hand. As he looked around the room he was relieved to see that about twenty-five medical staff, mostly doctors, but a few of the senior nurses had turned up this morning. The meeting wasn't compulsory but it was to everyone's advantage that as many people as possible attended so that they could report back to their various departments.

He was very much aware that Lucy's eyes were fixed on him but he had to put her out of his mind on a personal level for the moment.

'*Si, Dottore?*' he said quickly as one of his junior colleagues raised a hand.

'Vittorio, I thought everybody would like to know that there has been a breakthrough in the case of Alfredo

Fontana. He's the man who fell from his balcony and was admitted two weeks ago suffering from a fractured skull.'

Vittorio nodded. 'We removed a large haematoma from the base of Alfredo's skull, didn't we? He's been in a coma ever since.'

'He came round early this morning!' the doctor said excitedly. 'We are all delighted in the department. He's undergoing tests on his brain at the moment but the indications are that the brain damage we initially suspected hasn't happened.'

Lucy found herself smiling with relief. 'That's excellent news,' she said, speaking carefully and clearly in Italian so that all her colleagues could hear and understand her. 'I've been following the case each day. Alfredo's wife was afraid he would never come round from the coma and if he did he might have changed completely. Was she with him when he regained consciousness, Dottore?'

The young doctor smiled and assured Lucy that Anastasia had hardly left her husband's bedside for two weeks.

'So, what other news do we have?' Vittorio continued.

Glancing down the long list of patients, he knew he would have to draw the meeting to a close very soon.

The nursing sister in charge of the ward where their patient Cecilia was being treated after her mastectomy reported that at the moment there were no more signs of cancer in her patient. She wanted to thank Dr Lucy for spotting the discharge from Cecilia's nipple after she'd been admitted with broken ribs.

Vittorio smiled. 'Yes, it's always important to remember in Pronto Soccorso that we must treat the patient as a whole. Sometimes an emergency patient may have other symptoms entirely unrelated to the immediate problem. *Grazie, Dottore Lucy.*'

'*Prego, Dottore Vittorio,*' she said, demurely lowering her eyes so that she didn't have to meet his gaze.

'Now, very quickly,' Vittorio said, in super efficient tones. 'I'll go down the list of patients and we'd like to hear of any significant changes in treatment or condition, *per favore.*'

Lucy listened attentively, taking notes on patients she'd admitted so she could continue to follow them up.

She heard that Queenie, the mischievous old lady who'd pretended she'd lost her memory, had gone home a couple of days ago after undergoing extensive tests to establish her state of mind. It had been decided that she was mentally above average for a woman of nearly eighty, although a little confused at times.

She'd actually wanted to stay on, having insisted on the best treatment possible in the ward, but she was finally persuaded to go home with her daughter who was becoming embarrassed by all the fuss and anxious to get her mother back to a more normal life.

'I'll have to call a halt to our meeting now,' Vittorio said. 'I've got to be in Theatre in a few minutes and I know that everybody here is needed in their various departments. Thank you for coming.'

Vittorio paused beside Lucy on his way out. She was talking animatedly to one of the other doctors from Pronto Soccorso.

'*Scusi, Dottore Lucy,*' he began. 'I've had a message from Carlos regarding arrangements in Pronto Soccorso during his coming leave of absence. He would like to see both of us at the end of the afternoon in his office, unless there's an emergency situation that we can't leave.'

'I'll be there,' Lucy said, in her super-professional voice.

She walked with her colleague towards the main assessment area. Several patients were waiting for attention. Sister called Lucy over to the first cubicle. Lucy went inside and looked down at the injured man lying on the examination couch as Sister filled her in on the details.

The injuries had been sustained in an industrial accident apparently. The man had been working on a machine and had failed to use safety precautions. Consequently, his hand was almost severed at the wrist.

Lucy stemmed the flow of blood with a tourniquet, set up a drip to rehydrate her patient and added a butterfly clip through which she could administer painkillers. Having dealt with the immediate emergency treatment required, she called Theatre. She was surprised when Vittorio answered.

'I was hoping to speak to Theatre Sister,' Lucy said quickly.

'I just happened to be passing her desk. She's with a patient at the moment. Can I give her a message?'

'I have a patient who needs immediate surgery to a partially severed hand.'

'Prepare your patient for Theatre, Lucy. I can fit him into my list immediately. My first patient has been delayed.'

'That's excellent! Thanks, Vittorio.'

'Give me some details. What's your patient's name?'

'Guiliano Ciameno.' Lucy grabbed the case notes she'd made, explaining everything that Vittorio would need to know before she hung up and began to prepare her patient for Theatre.

It had been a stroke of luck that Vittorio had answered

the phone. He was a totally dedicated surgeon who didn't mind fitting an extra patient into his list. And from the reports she'd heard about his surgical expertise, she knew his work was first class.

'The surgeon who's operating on you is excellent, Giuliano,' Lucy told her patient as she administered his pre-operative drug.

The young man looked up at her. 'Will I be able to play the piano when he's finished with me?'

'Do you play the piano?'

Giuliano grinned. 'Not yet, but I might like to learn, mightn't I?'

Lucy felt relieved that the man could joke at a time like this. He'd been in considerable pain when she'd first started treating him but he'd suffered without making a fuss.

'With an attitude like yours you're going to be fine,' Lucy said, checking on the sterile bandage she'd applied. Her tourniquet had stemmed the flow of blood but she would be relieved to hand her patient over to Vittorio.

In theatre, Vittorio began preparing for his operation on Giuliano Ciameno. A partially severed wrist was an intricate operation. Not only was there the difficulty of realigning the wrist bones, some of which would inevitably be fractured, he also had to ensure that the nerve and blood supply was reconnected between the arm and the hand. It was only marginally less difficult than attempting to reattach a totally severed hand.

But it was an operation he'd performed several times. He always hoped for total success but that depended on several factors. The general health of the patient could be important, and from what Lucy had told him, it appeared that her twenty-five-year old patient stood a good chance.

He'd contacted the neurological department and had been assured that a senior neurological surgeon would arrive in Theatre as soon as possible so that they could liaise about the damage to the nerves of the hand and arm.

The patient would arrive shortly. There was nothing more he had to do but prepare himself by scrubbing up and putting on his theatre garments. A nurse was standing by, holding a theatre gown ready for him.

'They're ready for you,' she said as she fixed the back of the gown and handed over a pair of sterile gloves.

Another nurse was holding back the swing doors. Vittorio was totally in command as he walked through and looked down at the unconscious patient. The theatre sister had removed the sterile bandage that Lucy had fixed in place. Vittorio examined the injured bones and tissues. It wasn't going to be easy but he was confident he could reattach the hand. Lucy had been quite right to insist on immediate surgery. In cases like this, the quicker the patient was operated on, the more chance there was of a successful outcome.

CHAPTER FIVE

'How did the operation on Guiliano's hand go?' Lucy asked Vittorio as he came into Carlos's office at the end of the afternoon.

Lucy and Carlos had been waiting several minutes until Vittorio could leave Theatre so they'd been chatting about Sarah and baby Charlotte. But now that Vittorio was here they could return to the business in hand.

'I'm hopeful it will be a success,' Vittorio said evenly as he sank down into one of the chairs at the side of Carlos's desk. 'I never like to commit myself to a prognosis until at least a week after the operation. There are so many things that could go wrong in the post-operative stage. Let's just say that I'm quietly confident.'

They were all speaking English which was nice and easy for Lucy after a day of non-stop Italian. She was finding now that her Italian was improving all the time, but it was always a relief to return to English at the end of the day.

Carlos leaned across his desk. 'OK, the business in hand is that I've been granted extended leave of absence so that I can not only have Sarah at home with me but we can also bring Charlotte home.'

'That's great news!' Lucy said.

'Yes, it is,' Carlos said. 'Great news for Sarah and me, but an extra workload for Vittorio. What I'm proposing to do is ask Vittorio which department he prefers to take charge of, Orthopaedics or Accident and

Emergency. I'll make arrangements for another consultant to be appointed to whichever department Vittorio
decides he will leave. Obviously, Vittorio, you will need
time to consider your decision so—'

'I've already decided,' Vittorio said.

'You have?' Carlos looked surprised. 'Well, what's it
to be?'

'Pronto Soccorso.'

'Are you absolutely sure?'

'Positive.'

Lucy could see that Vittorio was deliberately avoiding
her eyes. As she turned back to look at Carlos she wondered how much he'd deduced about her relationship
with Vittorio.

Carlos watched them carefully as he spoke again. 'I
know there were strong reasons why you changed from
Accident and Emergency to Orthopaedics in the hospital
where you were working in Milano so perhaps you
should give it more consideration, Vittorio.'

Vittorio shook his head. 'All that is now in the past.
I feel strong enough to work in Pronto Soccorso again.'

Lucy found herself wondering what these strong reasons had been which had caused Vittorio to leave
Accident and Emergency. Did Carlos know the details?
If so, he was making it perfectly obvious that he was
going to keep the secret he shared with Vittorio.

She suppressed a sigh as she thought that Vittorio was
one of the most mysterious men she'd ever encountered…apart from Mark. As the thought flashed through
her mind she felt a frisson of anxiety. There were areas
in Vittorio's background that she knew nothing about.
And it didn't seem likely that Vittorio would enlighten
her. If ever he felt she was becoming inquisitive about
his background he reverted to being the darkly brooding,

secretive, mysterious stranger she'd found him to be when they'd first met.

Carlos smiled knowingly as he glanced from Sarah to Vittorio. 'Is there any particular reason why you feel you can now move on, Vittorio?'

'My main concern is to do the best job I can in Accident and Emergency,' Vittorio said evenly.

'Of course,' Carlos said, moving swiftly on. 'I've been telling Lucy about the arrangements I've made to have Sarah and the baby at home with me. As you know, I've got an apartment here in Rome and a house down at the coast. I'm arranging to have a full-time trained nurse to live with us when baby Charlotte is able to come out of hospital. She's out of her incubator but is still underweight and will need round-the-clock supervision. The nurse will help Sarah and me to ensure that Charlotte gets the best treatment.'

'Sarah told me you're going to be based in the Rome apartment at first, aren't you?' Lucy said.

Carlos nodded. 'That's because we need to be near the hospital in case there is a problem with Charlotte that we can't deal with. As soon as she's stronger, we'll go down to the coast.'

He paused before continuing. 'Sarah and I would be delighted if the two of you came down to stay with us one weekend…'

Carlos's voice trailed away before he smiled and began again. 'I hope you don't mind me assuming that the pair of you would enjoy a weekend by the sea together?'

Vittorio swallowed hard. 'Carlos, are you trying to find out what's going on between Lucy and me?'

Carlos's mouth twitched. 'Nothing could be further from my mind, Vittorio! But I do hope my assumptions are correct. I've seen the two of you working together, noticed you going off duty together and…what is the English phrase? I've put two and two together?'

Vittorio leaned forward. 'Let's just say that Lucy and I are enjoying getting to know each other. But because of our past relationships neither of us want to commit to anything more than a light romance in the future.'

Vittorio glanced at Lucy. 'Is that how you see it, Lucy?'

She nodded. 'A light romance would seem to describe our situation.'

'That was exactly how Sarah and I started our romance,' Carlos put in quickly. 'And then we both found ourselves falling in love and—'

'Carlos, with the greatest respect,' Vittorio interrupted hastily, 'our situations are completely different, as you must realise.'

'If you say so,' Carlos said evenly. 'I'm sorry if I've embarrassed you by jumping to conclusions, Vittorio.'

Vittorio clenched his fists as he tried desperately to keep his cool. 'Not at all, Carlos. You and I have been friends and colleagues for a long time. I think we understand each other.'

As Vittorio stood up, Lucy noticed he was breathing heavily. Carlos's assumption that the two of them were planning a future together had obviously touched a raw nerve. Again it had become quite clear that Vittorio had no intention of committing to a permanent relationship ever again. That was what she herself had vowed in those dark days following her break-up with Mark, but she was finding it more and more difficult to check her feelings of deep attraction towards Vittorio.

As she followed Vittorio out of the room, she found herself wondering how long she could go on pretending that she hadn't fallen in love with him. And as there was no future for them together, shouldn't she be trying to rein in her emotions before she got in too deep?

During the next week, Lucy and Vittorio saw each other every day. Now that Vittorio was in charge of Pronto Soccorso full time, they found themselves working together or conferring about mutual patients more often.

But, perhaps conscious of the fact that there had been speculation about their relationship, Vittorio had remained utterly professional when they worked together. As the week progressed, Lucy felt that Vittorio seemed to be trying to cool things down between them.

Possibly their one night of rapture had been a mistake for both of them. As the days passed, this was the conclusion she reached. Vittorio must have been reconsidering the situation and had decided that they'd gone further than they should, given that neither of them wanted to commit to a heavy relationship.

But every time she was near Vittorio, she felt a magnetic pull towards him. She couldn't help the frissons of excitement as his hand accidentally touched hers when they were working on a case together. Her frustration was mounting as the days progressed and she longed to be alone again with him, even though she might find it emotionally dangerous.

So, at the end of the week, she plucked up courage and casually asked Vittorio if he would like to go to the cinema with her. She'd thought the whole thing through before she made the suggestion as they were both leaving at the end of a long day. This was what light romances were all about, wasn't it?

Vittorio seemed taken aback. 'What's the film about?'

'It's an English film taken from a book by Jane Austen,' she said quickly. '*Sense and Sensibility*. It's in

English but there are Italian subtitles...not that you'll need them...'

Her voice trailed away as she watched his reaction.

As Vittorio smiled, Lucy found herself relaxing again.

'Oh, I think I might need subtitles.' He paused. 'But are you sure you really want me to go with you?'

Her heart was thudding. They were walking quickly along the corridor that led to the residents' quarters. A couple of medical colleagues were coming towards them. She wished they were having this conversation in private. There was so much to be said, but a hospital corridor wasn't the right place.

'Why not?' she asked.

'Well, we've both been a bit distant with each other this week, haven't we?'

'I assumed you were trying to cool things down between us.'

'Possibly I was,' Vittorio said carefully. 'It was when Carlos made the assumption that we were heading for—'

'I know! I've known Carlos much longer than you and he's a true romantic.'

Vittorio stopped in the corridor, putting a hand on her arm to detain her. 'So am I,' he said huskily. 'But I do believe that our romance is different. We're both still trying to forget the past. I'd like us to live in the present, you and I. Enjoy each moment we spend together, without looking too far into the future. Isn't that what you would like, too?'

Lucy looked up into his dark, expressive eyes. 'Yes, that's what I want.'

'So that's what we'll have.' Vittorio bent his head and kissed her on the lips.

She savoured the touch of his lips in that brief moment. As she raised her head, she noticed that Vittorio had already glanced along the corridor to see if anyone was watching. The corridor was deserted.

She wondered briefly how long she would be able to be part of a temporary relationship like this. One where only the present mattered. Was she making another disastrous mistake?

If she could hold onto her deep emotions, if she could prevent herself from falling in love with Vittorio, she could enjoy this light-hearted affair she was having. But if she got in too deep she would suffer when the affair ended. Was the risk worth taking?

'I'll meet you in Reception in half an hour,' she said quickly.

As they went into the cinema together, Lucy could feel that they'd set the mood just right that evening. They'd chatted non-stop in the taxi, laughed a great deal at the amusing incidents that each of them had recounted concerning hospital life. Their slight rift of the previous week had been replaced as they both attempted to enjoy the moment.

There was barely time to settle into their seats before the film started. Lucy always found it amusing when she was waiting for the subtitles to appear on the screen to see if they matched up to what the actors were saying. But in the poignant scene where it seemed as if the two lovers were doomed to remain apart she found herself scrabbling in her bag in search of a tissue as she tried to stop sniffing.

'I'm sure they'll get together at the end,' Vittorio whispered as he passed Lucy a clean handkerchief.

Lucy dabbed her eyes as she whispered her reply. 'You're right. I've read the book so I know it's got a happy ending. I only like films with happy endings.'

'What about real life?' Vittorio whispered.

'Let's not go into that now,' she said, barely audible under her breath.

For the moment she wanted to immerse herself in the fictitious problems in the film. She didn't want to look too far ahead in her real life. The present was wonderful. She would deal with future problems when they arose.

Vittorio reached for her hand. He, too, was enjoying this respite from the cares of the world. He'd forced himself to stop wondering if the night staff were doing regular checks on Giuliano. And then there was his personal life with Lucy. How long could he sustain the light affair he was enjoying so much without losing his heart?

The film was drawing to a close. The lights came up again, everybody blinking and squinting in the brightness. Lucy was bending down, searching for Vittorio's handkerchief, which she thought she must have dropped on the floor.

'It doesn't matter.' Vittorio took her hand.

'Here it is! I'll wash it for you.' Lucy stuffed the handkerchief in her bag.

They went outside and decided to walk back to the hospital. The delicious aroma from a pizzeria near the hospital was very tempting. Vittorio asked Lucy if she'd share a pizza with him back in his rooms. Lucy said she was starving and would be delighted.

They arrived back in the residents' quarters and went into Vittorio's kitchen, carrying supper in a large paper package.

'I'll open the wine,' Vittorio said, reaching for a corkscrew.

'Anything I can do?' Lucy asked, as she took a couple of plates from one of the shelves.

'Would you like to make a salad?'

'Sure.' Lucy opened the fridge and reached inside in search of lettuce and whatever else she could find. There was an enormous round misshapen Italian tomato and some olives. She took the whole lot over to the sink.

'I'll put your wineglass here on the table.'

'Thanks.'

Lucy took a sip before beginning to wash the lettuce. She was enjoying the easy going rapport that existed between them this evening and hoped that they could sustain it.

Vittorio was now standing beside her at the sink, stirring a vinaigrette dressing for the salad. She turned her head and smiled up at him. He put down the bowl he was holding and took her in his arms. Gently he lowered his head and kissed her very slowly and so tenderly that it almost took her breath away. As she opened her eyes she saw the wonderful expression in his. They were already lovers in the true sense of the word. She could feel the warm vibrancy flowing between them.

These were the moments she was going to enjoy. Light, simple moments that re-established what they had between them. An uncomplicated romance that would one day have to end. She was happy to settle for that…wasn't she?

If that was all that was possible. She turned away and took the bowl of salad to the table.

Vittorio poured the dressing over it and Lucy began to turn the salad with the large wooden servers she'd found in the drawer of the table.

'It's an enormous pizza!' Lucy said, as Vittorio reached for a knife. 'It didn't look quite so big in the pizzeria.'

Vittorio laughed. 'Ah, yes, we Italians never do things by halves.'

'I'll have a small portion to begin with— Oh, not so big!'

'You can leave it if that's too much.' Vittorio picked up the wine bottle and topped up her glass. 'All we need now is some background music...'

He moved across the kitchen to select something. As the first haunting notes of the music floated across the kitchen Lucy recognised it at once.

'Puccini,' she said, swallowing a mouthful of the delicious pizza.

Vittorio resumed his seat at the table. 'I know you enjoyed *La Boheme* when we were at the opera together. I've given you a scene near the beginning where Rudolpho and Mimi are still happy.'

Lucy smiled. 'You've gathered that I find the sad scenes difficult to take.'

Vittorio reached across the table and covered her hand with his. 'So do I. I'd much rather have a happy ending...but that's not always possible, is it?'

'No, it's not. We have to take life as it comes, don't we?'

Vittorio nodded.

Their eyes locked for a few moments. The combination of the haunting music and the tender expression in Vittorio's eyes was becoming too poignant for Lucy. She looked down at her plate.

'I'm enjoying the pizza,' she said brightly.

'Do you think you'll be able to finish it?' Vittorio said.

'Oh, I'm sure I will.' She swallowed hard. 'I love this part of the music where Rudolpho comes in and begins...'

She chattered on, deliberately immersing herself in the music. Vittorio joined in the discussion. She realised that she and Vittorio had a lot in common—a love of music, opera, films, books. They enjoyed walking together beside the river or through the picturesque streets of Rome. They shared the same profession. In every respect they would make an ideal couple. Except for the fact that neither of them wanted to be part of a couple again.

At least, Vittorio didn't. She was beginning to have serious doubts about the resolutions she'd made when she'd discovered Mark's treachery. Surely, she would dare to trust Vittorio…if only…

Lucy looked across at the dark, wonderfully expressive eyes and felt the now familiar arousal of longing deep down inside her.

She couldn't imagine life without him now. It had been a whirlwind romance so far. She was trying to convince herself that this was all she wanted but she knew she wanted more.

Vittorio stood up and came round the table, his eyes full of concern. 'I can see that something is troubling you.'

He drew her to her feet and gazed down at her with such tenderness that she could feel her legs turning to jelly.

'It's the music,' she said in a wavering voice. 'This section always has that effect on me.'

Slowly Vittorio lowered his head until their lips were touching. Lucy parted her lips, waiting for the tantalising excitement of Vittorio's kiss. His lips hovered gently close to hers for a few moments before his kiss deepened. Lucy sighed as erotic sensations began to surge through her body.

Lucy had no idea how long they remained locked in each other's arms before Vittorio pulled himself away and looked down at her, his eyes searching her face.

'It's something more than the music, I think,' he said.

Lucy shook her head. 'I'm perfectly happy. This is the happiest I've been since…' She broke off as her voice choked.

'You can't forget that love rat, can you?' Vittorio said. 'Have you told me everything about him?'

'Of course not! It was all too—'

'Don't you think it would help if you unburdened yourself to me?' Vittorio said, his voice husky with emotion.

Lucy swallowed hard. She wanted so much to confide in him. His wonderfully expressive eyes were giving her such comfort as she gazed up at him.

'It might,' she said in a small voice. Maybe it was time she confided more in Vittorio, even though his background was a closed book to her.

He put an arm around her shoulders and drew her out through the kitchen door into the living room. Gently guiding her down onto the sofa, he dabbed at her damp cheeks with a tissue.

She looked up at him, loving the expression of tenderness on his face, wondering whether or not she dared to tell him the depths of her anguish when she'd miscarried.

'I became pregnant when I was with Mark,' she said quietly. 'I was overjoyed when I discovered I was expecting a baby, but at three months I had a miscarriage.'

She swallowed hard. 'I'm not going to cry again, Vittorio, I'm not going to…'

But the tears were already rolling down her cheeks. Vittorio held her against him, his hands stroking the back of her hair with gentle sympathetic caresses.

'You poor darling. Cry as much as you like, Lucy,' he murmured. 'Everybody needs to grieve. In time you won't grieve for your baby any more. You'll remember the loss, but the grief will have been taken away.'

She looked up into his eyes. 'Do you really think so? How can you be so sure?'

Vittorio sighed. 'I know so.' He paused before taking a deep breath. 'I lost my baby son when he was nine months old.'

'No! Oh, Vittorio I'm so sorry. I had no idea...'

'As I say, I've stopped grieving. Sometimes you need the help of another person...someone who is close to you. Since I got to know you, Lucy, I've been able to stop grieving. Let me help you as you've helped me.'

'Vittorio, if you've stopped grieving, do you feel able to move on?'

A veiled expression came over his eyes. 'Yes and no. I've stopped grieving but I wouldn't ever want to go through that again. I daren't risk the pain of losing family.'

For a moment Lucy felt she'd glimpsed the real Vittorio. She was beginning to understand why he was so adamant that he couldn't commit to another close relationship. The loss she felt for her unborn baby was bad enough, but to have actually had a living, breathing child who had died was unimaginable.

'Vittorio, just hold me in your arms' she whispered, snuggling closer to him. 'That's the only help I need at the moment. Just feeling you close to me. Let's stop thinking about the sadness in our pasts. We've got each other, which is all that matters for the moment.'

As he drew her closer, she raised her eyes to his. 'Take me to bed, Vittorio. Make love to me. I want to lose myself in—'

His lips claimed hers. Hungrily, she savoured the taste of his tongue, clinging to him as if her life depended on it. She sighed as she realised she was about to embark on another journey into ecstasy. That was as far as she could think at the moment. There was no yesterday, no tomorrow, just the present moment…

Later, much later, as she opened her eyes, her body still tingling from their ecstatic love-making, she gave a sigh of contentment. She was already lowering herself gently down to earth. She'd been floating on cloud nine but it was now time to return to the real world.

She turned her head on the pillow. By the light of the early morning sun streaming through the windows she saw that Vittorio was no longer there. She put out an exploratory hand to see if he was snuggled down under the sheet somewhere but his side of the bed was empty.

'Vittorio!' She felt an irrational moment of panic at finding herself alone in his bed.

'*Buon giorno, cara mia.*' Vittorio came through the door, carrying a huge tray of food. There was a candle in the middle of the tray which illuminated the small vase holding a rose that was balanced precariously near it.

Lucy smiled as she pulled herself into a sitting position. 'I wasn't aware I'd called room service.'

Vittorio grinned. 'I made the call myself…to my own kitchen. I requested toasted focaccia, coffee and fruit. But as nobody answered I went down to help myself. Does the *signorina* approve of my choice?'

'Absolutely!'

She also approved of the sexy way that Vittorio undid the belt of his robe, allowing it to slip to the floor as he set the tray down on a small table. His tanned skin, the rippling of his muscles was almost taking away her ap-

petite for food again. She felt very hungry but the sight
of Vittorio's body was food enough!

She forced herself to control her appetite for more of
the erotic delights they'd enjoyed together during the
night. Vittorio placed the tray between them on the
covers so they could help themselves. As Lucy propped
herself against the pillows she felt a surge of happiness
stealing over her.

Losing herself in the delights of making love with
Vittorio had released all her tension. Yes, she'd stopped
grieving. But unlike Vittorio she had come to believe
that it would be worth taking a risk on true love again.
That was where they differed now.

Vittorio lifted the tray onto his bedside table and
leaned back against the pillows. Lucy looked so wonderful this morning, with her long blonde hair tumbling
everywhere like spun gold over the pillow. He would
like to take that dreadful man who'd caused her so much
pain and tear him limb from limb!

He took a deep breath to steady his growing anger at
the intolerable situation that man had been responsible
for.

'Had Mark wanted the baby?' he asked, in as con-
trolled a manner as he could manage, considering how
he was feeling.

'It was Mark's suggestion that we try for a family
together.'

'The swine! You told me he already had a family!
How on earth could he think that—?'

'Vittorio, Mark was living in a fantasy world, escap-
ing from the demands of his real life family.'

'That's no excuse!'

Vittorio took another deep breath. He could see that

his reaction was upsetting Lucy and that was the last thing he wanted to do.

'What was Mark's reaction when you told him you were pregnant?' he said evenly.

'I didn't tell him. I was planning to tell him around the time that I discovered his treachery. I couldn't tell him once I discovered how he'd deluded me into thinking he was a free man.'

'Instead of a man who should have shouldered his domestic responsibilities to his family,' Vittorio interrupted, breathing heavily with outrage at a man who could deceive his wife and family.

He leaned back against the pillows and put his hands behind his head, staring up at the ceiling as he realised he couldn't contemplate how any man could behave in such a despicable manner.

'Your boyfriend was a scoundrel!' Vittorio said. 'He simply wanted a good time, regardless of who he hurt in the process. You must have been devastated when you realised that you would have to have the baby by yourself.'

Lucy hesitated. 'At first, yes. But I realised that I loved my baby for itself, not for who its father was. I channelled all my love towards my baby.'

She swung her legs over the side of the bed. The time for grieving was over. It was time to move on.

Vittorio put out a hand. 'Don't go yet, Lucy.'

'I must,' she said. 'I don't want anyone to see me leaving your room.'

As she hurried away she was hoping that Vittorio might say it didn't matter. But there was no response.

As Vittorio walked into his office the phone on his desk was ringing. *'Pronto! Vittorio Vincenzi... Si...'*

He put down the phone and reached for his stethoscope. Yet another car crash on the busy road beside the Tiber! When would these idiots learn to slow down? He pressed the red button indicating another emergency as he hurried out into the assessment area.

Lucy was already there, looking after a small child who'd been brought in on a stretcher.

Lucy looked up, one hand still soothing her crying patient. 'What's the emergency, Vittorio?'

'Another car crash. I'll pull in some extra staff from other departments.'

'I'll finish treating my little patient and then I'm available,' Lucy said as she smiled down at the small boy. 'Now, tell me what happened to you after you fell off the wall, Niko.'

Seven-year-old Niko told Lucy his leg had gone all floppy. He couldn't walk and it hurt a lot. He'd lain on the ground shouting until somebody had phoned for an ambulance. His mother didn't know he was there and he didn't want her to be told. He shouldn't have been in that garden. His mother had told him not to go stealing grapes any more.

'I didn't intend to steal a lot of grapes,' Niko said in his serious, charming Italian. 'Just a few for my friend and me.'

'Where is your friend?' Lucy asked.

'He stayed on the other side of the wall. It's a high, very high wall and I can climb better than he can. If anybody comes I can escape quickly.'

'Well, let's have a look at your leg, Niko. Would you like to wipe your face?' She handed the young boy a piece of damp gauze. It would be much easier to do it herself but she didn't want to hurt his young pride. She

watched as he attempted to remove the dirty streaks from
his tear-stained face.

He was a dear little scalliwag! Her heart went out to
him as he struggled to become tough again. She would
have his leg X-rayed soon but glancing down, seeing the
protrusion of the tibia through the skin with the fibula
close behind, she could make her own immediate diagnosis. Poor little lamb. Fractures of the tibia and fibula
would take weeks of good orthopaedic care to produce
effective healing.

Lucy ran her fingers lightly over the injured limb, not-
ing the displacement. As soon as she could get Vittorio's
attention again she would ask him to liaise with the orthopaedic department. Meanwhile she would ensure that
the limb was immobilised on an orthopaedic slab before
her patient was transferred to the primary orthopaedic
unit.

Lucy scribbled her instructions on the appropriate
forms, explaining to the nurse who was assisting her
what she required.

'Niko, Nurse is going to take you to the X-ray department now. They'll take a picture of your leg. Then
you'll go to a nice little ward. Nurse will stay with you
until you're settled in. Now, I'm going to ask somebody
to call your mother because—'

'I don't want my—'

'Niko, your mother will be worried when you don't
come home. She'll be really kind to you when she sees
that you've hurt your leg, I'm sure. I'm glad you're
seven years big, because I'm sure you can remember
your telephone number, can't you?'

'Of course I can,' Niko said.

Lucy wrote down the number as her patient reeled
it off.

'Thank you, Niko. I'll get someone to call your mother. Now, don't worry, will you? We'll tell Mamma you've been a big brave boy and she'll be very proud of you.'

The injured people from the car crash had arrived and were being treated in the order that their condition determined. From the four-car pile-up, nine people had been ferried to hospital in ambulances. Two, unfortunately, were dead on arrival and were transferred to the mortuary as soon as their relatives had been informed. One patient whom Lucy treated for a head injury died shortly after arrival.

As she looked down at the pale, motionless body of the young man she'd battled to save, Lucy felt a shiver of sadness running through her. What a terrible, useless, unnecessary…

She looked up as Vittorio came into the cubicle. 'I've checked everything, but there's no sign of life,' she said, her voice cracking with the stress of the ordeal she'd just faced.

She took a deep breath as she tried to take control of her emotions. 'There's nothing more I have to do but sign the death certificate…'

Her self-imposed composure began to crack as she reached inside her white coat for her pen. 'What a waste of a young life! Why did it happen? Why do young drivers treat roads as if they were race tracks? I hate it when a patient dies on me! A patient I'd desperately wanted to save. I always feel I could have done more and yet…'

Vittorio drew her against him and held her close for a moment before releasing her.

'You did all you could. The skull was too badly smashed. The brain had been utterly crushed. Let it go.'

Lucy pulled herself away as she absorbed the logic of Vittorio's comforting words.

'I suppose you're right. I wanted to play God, to change an impossible situation…but you can't do that can you?'

Her momentary lapse from being professional was over. In emergency situations you couldn't afford yourself the luxury of feeling too deeply for your patients. If you did you would be in a permanent emotional state of exhaustion. She would try to forget the patient who hadn't survived and concentrate on those who had.

'Vittorio, have you had time to examine little Niko, the boy with the fractured tib and fib I told you about?'

Vittorio nodded. 'Niko is on his way to Theatre. The new orthopaedic consultant who's taken over from me is going to operate on him.'

'Thanks. Poor little boy. Did his mother arrive?'

'She arrived just in time to sign the consent form.'

Lucy smiled. 'And was she furious with Niko?'

Vittorio smiled back. 'She was a charming, well-groomed, intelligent lady, her only concern being that her son should survive his ordeal. She cuddled him—much to his disgust, I might add!—and told him he'd been a brave boy. She told me when Niko wasn't listening that she was concerned that he was turning into a bit of a tearaway but I assured her he would grow out of it. I remember my mother saying the same about me and look how I turned out!'

Lucy smiled. 'I'm not sure how to take that. I'd have loved to have seen you when you were a boy. I'd have loved to…'

She broke off as her imagination got the better of her.

In her mind's eye she could see a charming little Italian scalliwag who deeply resembled his handsome father. She felt the deep, unrelenting pull of her maternal instincts. She would have loved the child she hadn't managed to carry to full term. But even more she would love to bear a child for Vittorio. But that was one dream that was never going to happen.

'OK, I'd better get on,' she said briskly, as gently and reverently she pulled a sheet over her dead patient's face. 'I'll just sign this death certificate before I hand over to…'

'There's one of the car crash victims waiting to be seen by a doctor in the next cubicle,' Vittorio said, turning as he went towards the door. 'His name is Rinaldo. Provisional diagnosis pre-X-ray is fractured spine, damage to right arm and foot. Clinical case notes are with the patient. *Arrivederci…*'

Vittorio hurried away.

Lucy nodded as she scribbled her signature on the death certificate.

By the end of the day, Lucy had been directly involved with most of the patients who'd been admitted as a direct result of the car pile-up. After fixing Rinaldo, her patient with the fractured spine, in traction, she'd had him transferred directly to the orthopaedic ward where he would receive specialised treatment for his other injures.

The ulna and scaphoid in Rinaldo's right arm and wrist were fractured and his right foot was injured in several places. In his foot, the metatarsals had all fractured and the calcaneus, the heel bone, had been shattered when he'd pressed down on the brake in an effort to stop his car hurtling into the car in front. In the inevitable impact the engine had come through and badly damaged his foot .

'You're lucky to be alive,' Lucy told the young man as she checked on his condition before going off duty. 'Somebody up there must have been taking care of you today.'

Rinaldo looked up at her, his neck pinned down against the orthopaedic bed. 'I don't feel very alive at the moment, Lucy. One of the straps holding my neck in place is pulling on my hair. I only noticed it when the morphine started wearing off. Do you think you can fix it for me?'

Lucy leaned forward and eased one of the straps of the neck brace. Poor Rinaldo, she thought as she looked down at him. She couldn't imagine how awful it would be to be lying still like that, unable to move. She felt almost guilty at being able to escape into the big wide world again for another exciting night with Vittorio.

As if he'd sensed she was thinking about him, Vittorio came through the door of the primary care unit.

'I'm surprised you're still here, Lucy. You should have been off duty an hour ago.'

'I'm just coming.'

'If you two are going out tonight, will you take me with you?' the young patient joked with remarkable sto-icism considering the dire situation he was in.

Vittorio leaned over their patient. 'Sorry, Rinaldo. Not tonight. Is anybody coming to see you?'

Rinaldo gave a brave smile. 'My girlfriend, I hope. I'm planning to jump out of bed and surprise her. I thought we might have a walk down by the river, go to the cinema…something like that…'

Vittorio patted Rinaldo's hand. 'You'll soon be doing just that. There's no irreparable damage to your spine, which was our main concern. The bones in your foot will heal and your arm won't present a major problem. As soon as the vertebrae heal you'll be up and about.'

'*Grazie*, Vittorio.'

'Well, are you ready, Lucy?'

As they walked down the ward, Vittorio asked if she had any plans for the evening.

'I'm planning on staying in and having an early night,' she said as they walked out into the corridor.

'Well, why don't you come round first and let me cook something? I was thinking of staying in this evening.' Vittorio smiled. 'We could stay in together.'

Lucy hesitated. 'You come to my place. I'll cook something. I can cook, you know.'

'I'm sure you can. I accept your invitation. I'll be with you in…what shall we say, half an hour?'

'Come round whenever you like, Vittorio. I'll leave the door unlocked in case I'm still in the shower.'

Vittorio cupped her face in his hands and kissed her gently on the lips. 'In that case I'll be with you as soon as soon as I can.'

As he smiled down at her, Lucy felt the familiar excitement of knowing that another wonderful evening with Vittorio was beginning. She wanted a quiet evening with her lover. The bright lights of Rome were fun but tonight it would be just the two of them.

She hurried into her room, tossing her clothes on the bed as she went across to the little shower room. As the warm water began to caress her skin she heard the sound of Vittorio's footsteps crossing the living room.

'I'm in the shower,' she called. 'Come and join me, Vittorio…'

She gasped as she saw he had taken her quite literally, appearing at the door to the tiny shower room, a towel tied around his waist. She laughed as he attempted to join her in the tiny shower cubicle.

'This shower wasn't made for two people,' Lucy said, stepping out and reaching for her towel.

Vittorio drew her against him. 'Mmm, you smell so good.'

Her towel slid to the floor. As she reached up to kiss Vittorio she wondered just how long this ephemeral magic could last. She had to make the most of every precious moment they were together because it couldn't last much longer…

CHAPTER SIX

IT WAS way after midnight when Vittorio returned to his room. Every sensory nerve in his body had been urging him to stay all night in Lucy's bed but his head was telling him he should remain totally sensible and focused. The night staff were prone to phoning his room and even though he was technically off duty he still felt he didn't want to miss a call that could be a matter of life or death.

As a matter of self-preservation he'd only given out his mobile number to close friends and colleagues so that his room number was the one that was most often used by vulnerable junior members of staff. And he couldn't help remembering the days when he'd been a junior, desperately grateful for advice from a more experienced doctor.

He lay back on his bed, his body tingling in the aftermath of making love with Lucy. He'd never imagined he could feel like this about another woman after Lavinia had died. But the difficulty was that he still felt he couldn't risk committing himself totally to Lucy.

If he lived with her for any length of time, he knew he would come to love her too much. Supposing she decided to leave him, to go back to England? And he couldn't bear it if anything ever happened to take her away from him. The only course of action that wasn't risky was to go on as they were doing. Enjoying each other's company, simply being lovers, not looking too far ahead.

Lucy seemed happy with the situation. She, too, had suffered, hadn't she? He remembered the anguish in her voice when she'd spoken about the baby she'd miscarried. He could tell that she adored children and would have made a perfect mother.

As for himself, after Ricardo had died he'd thought he would never recover. But life had gone on and he'd accepted the situation now. He'd loved the brief period when he'd been a father. Family had been everything to him.

He remembered his own childhood, being brought up by loving parents, having the constant joyful interaction with his brothers and sisters. Little Ricardo had been too young to enjoy that before he'd died. He'd hoped to create a large, loving family, a whole Vincenzi empire! But that wasn't to be. Unless…

Was he being given a second chance? Did he dare to risk loving Lucy and asking her to marry him? As soon as the idea emerged he dismissed it. Lucy didn't dare to commit herself again any more than he did. And even if she did, loving children as she did, she deserved to have someone who could father a child.

And he couldn't. Not after the vasectomy he'd been asked to undertake by Lavinia's obstetrician. He remembered how his surgical colleague had delivered the ultimatum shortly after Ricardo's difficult birth. Lavinia must never have any more children, he'd been told. And she wasn't strong enough to undergo any more surgery for a long time.

He remembered how he'd willingly undergone the operation. It had been his duty. So, as an infertile man, it wouldn't be fair to ask any woman who loved children to contemplate a long-term relationship.

As he mused further he was trying to convince himself

that he didn't want to change the tenor of the relationship he had with Lucy. But the more he thought about it, the more he realised that if he were to overcome his fear of commitment, it would be a good idea to investigate the possibility of a vasectomy reversal.

As he turned out the bedside light, he knew that his ideas were changing. He promised himself he would make some discreet enquiries. Whatever the chances of success, he would go through with it. The prospect that the vasectomy couldn't be reversed was very real in many cases that he knew of. It had been six years since his semen had contained the sperm that could fertilise a female egg.

If he found the operation was successful he would be in a position to ask Lucy to marry him. If he could overcome his fear of risking marriage and commitment again. But if it was unsuccessful, if the vasectomy couldn't be reversed, he would accept it. He had no right to impose himself on Lucy when she could have another chance of bearing children with a man who was fertile.

It was a hot night, the breeze from the river barely stirring the air in his room as it came through the open windows. He moved the sheet to one side so that he could feel the cooler air on his skin. As he did so the faint aroma of Lucy's scent came from the sheets where they'd made love the previous night, locked in each other's arms as they'd slept for short sessions between their love-making.

'Lucy, ah, Lucy,' he whispered huskily. 'I love you so much.'

He swallowed hard. It was true. He did love her. But he daren't tell her. He'd been pretending to himself that they were simply light-hearted lovers. Would he ever dare to tell her his true feelings?

Now that he'd decided to take the necessary steps towards a vasectomy reversal he knew that the longer he left it the more difficult the operation would be. He had to think now of the practicalities of his situation, given that he was a full-time doctor.

It would be impossible to have the operation here at the Ospedale Tevere without someone on the staff divulging his secret. He would have to go to Milano to see one of his colleagues there. He knew just the man! Luciano, a good friend from medical school, ran a fertility clinic. Nobody need know where he was, but he'd have to find a legitimate excuse for taking a week off work.

Tomorrow morning early he would phone Carlos at his apartment and ask him if he could come into the hospital for a short meeting with him.

'So, why all the secrecy, Vittorio?' Carlos asked in rapid, clipped tones as he looked across the desk in Vittorio's office.

'First of all, let me thank you for coming, Carlos. I'll explain why our meeting must be totally confidential,' Vittorio began, before hesitating as he tried to phrase his words carefully.

It was a sensitive subject and he had to tread carefully. Carlos was Lucy's sister's partner and would soon become her husband. He was also a very influential and distinguished figure at the Ospedale Tevere.

Carlos leaned forward. 'I came as soon as I could this morning. It sounded urgent and, as you insisted over the phone, I haven't told anybody that you've asked to see me. Is it something to do with your job, Vittorio? I'm glad that you were able to take over from me but if you're finding...'

Vittorio assured Carlos that it had nothing to do with his work. 'I'm enjoying the job. I need your advice about…about a rather delicate personal matter.'

Carlos leaned back in his chair, clasping his hands on the desk in front of him.

'That wouldn't be something to do with my soon-to-be sister-in-law would it?'

Vittorio cleared his throat. 'In a way, yes. When I spoke to you before and you asked about our relationship, I told you it was simply a light-hearted romance. That was all I intended it to be. But the more I get to know Lucy, the more I realise that I would be foolish not to risk loving her…in a more permanent way.'

'Exactly! The two of you seem made for each other.'

'Carlos, I realise that. The point is, dare I become part of a couple again? Dare I risk losing everything if—'

'Vittorio, nothing in life is ever certain. Situations change all the time. You can only be sure of the present moment. But I tell you this, sooner or later you will regret it if you don't make a more permanent arrangement with Lucy. That is, if she wishes to change from an affair.'

'I know, I know, I'm assuming too much. This is why I'm here now. I don't think I have the right to ask Lucy to marry me at the moment. You see, I had a vasectomy six years ago. I know Lucy loves children. If ever she contemplated marriage she would want a man who was fertile. So I've decided to investigate the possibility of have a vasectomy reversal.'

'I see.' Carlos's expression became more serious. 'And have you discussed this with Lucy?'

'No! Lucy mustn't know. She doesn't even know that I'm beginning to think about a more permanent relationship. I need to be completely clear in my own head that this is right for both of us.'

'I agree that it would be better not to tell Lucy that you are going ahead with a vasectomy reversal,' Carlos said quietly. 'Especially as you're still not sure if you would dare to marry again. As you say, it is much better that you should know the outcome, whatever that might be. How can I help?'

'I need to spend a week in Milano and I would prefer that my reason for going there doesn't have to be disclosed.'

Carlos frowned. 'Why do you have to go to Milano for the operation?'

'I have a friend who is the director of a fertility clinic. He would be extremely discreet, whereas I'm not sure what would come out on the hospital grapevine if I had the operation here.'

Carlos nodded. 'I see your point. Well, why don't we say that you have to go to Milano because of a family health problem? That is perfectly true. We are considering the health of your family, aren't we? In this case, any future family you might have, but that's of no concern to the hospital board.'

'Would my leave be granted on those grounds, Carlos?'

'Of course. The board won't question my terminology when I fill in the leave of absence form. Family health is of paramount importance here in Rome, just as it is in Milano.'

Vittorio gave a relieved smile. 'Excellent!'

'Leave it with me, Vittorio. I'll arrange the necessary paperwork. Now, let me see… We'll need to have your work covered for a week. If you can organise your operation to take place within the next two weeks I'll be able to come in myself and take charge of Pronto Soccorso again.'

'In the next two weeks?' Vittorio queried.

'As you know, Sarah and I are living in our apartment here in Rome. Baby Charlotte is still here in the special care baby unit. Within the next two weeks she should be strong enough to leave hospital and I want to be at home with Sarah when that happens.'

'Of course. Thanks very much, Carlos. And, please, not a word to Lucy or even to Sarah. Sisters, especially twins as close as Sarah and Lucy, tend to pass on information to each other, don't they?'

'Not a word,' Carlos said, standing up and holding out his hand. 'Good luck.'

The two men shook hands.

Carlos walked towards the door, then turned back and placed both hands on the desk in front of Vittorio.

'Vittorio, why don't you pick up the phone now and see if you can arrange something with your friend as soon as possible? The sooner I have to cover for you the better as far as I'm concerned. I would prefer to cover for you myself than have to nominate another member of staff.'

Vittorio took a deep breath. Events were moving too quickly now. He'd only decided last night to go ahead with the operation. But he had to look at it from Carlos's point of view. It made sense to go to Milano as soon as possible.

'Will you be able to get my leave of absence sanctioned quickly?'

Carlos smiled. 'No problem. I'll work on it as soon as you give me a date.'

'I'll phone Luciano now,' Vittorio said decisively, as he keyed in the necessary information on his computer so that he could search his address file for the number he needed. 'Do you have time to wait, Carlos?'

Carlos glanced at his watch. 'I have a few minutes.'

He walked away from the desk and sat down in an easy chair beside the window where the noise from the hospital forecourt outside would partially block out Vittorio's conversation. He didn't want to appear as if he was listening in as he picked up one of the medical magazines that were stacked on the coffee-table.

Flicking through the pages, he found it difficult to concentrate. He wanted so much for Vittorio to be successful in his operation. He could hear him talking now in the background but he deliberately blocked it out. This was a personal matter between Vittorio and the surgeon.

Carlos remembered how concerned he'd been when Vittorio had arrived to take over as orthopaedic consultant. Vittorio was an excellent consultant, highly efficient, deeply respected for the surgery he performed. He worked long hours, much longer than he was supposed to do. He seemed to want to immerse himself in something where he didn't have to think about his tragic personal life.

When he'd finally confided some of the details about the tragedy of his wife and child, Carlos had understood the reason for Vittorio's sadness. But now, within a few weeks of meeting Lucy, he was a completely new man. That's what love did for you! He wanted Vittorio to experience the close long-term commitment that he and Sarah shared.

But would Vittorio, given what he'd been through, be able to take such a big step and would Lucy accept if he proposed? It certainly seemed that Vittorio was now moving in the right direction but he had no idea how Lucy would react.

He would do whatever it took to make sure that Vittorio went ahead with the operation as soon as possible. He'd promised Sarah he would go to see baby Charlotte in the special care baby unit before hurrying back to the apartment. But he would stay here until—

'It's all arranged,' Vittorio announced.

'Well, that was quick,' Carlos said as he put down the magazine and walked over to sit down beside the desk. 'When are you going to Milano?'

'Tomorrow!'

'Tomorrow?'

Carlos found himself mentally trying to rearrange his schedule for the next week but he didn't want to worry Vittorio with the details.

'Can you arrange to cover for me from tomorrow, Carlos?'

'Of course. No problem. I'll contact the hospital board this morning and explain that I'll be covering for you for the next week.'

'I can't thank you enough.'

Carlos stood up. 'Going ahead with the operation is thanks enough for me, Vittorio. I really want to see you and Lucy as happy as Sarah and I.'

Vittorio swallowed hard as he watched Carlos leaving. The reality of what he was doing was now beginning to set in. As the door closed behind Carlos he looked down at the notes he'd jotted on his notepad while he'd discussed the situation with Luciano.

He'd been lucky to have caught Luciano between consultations. His friend had explained that there was no guarantee that the operation would be a success. On that proviso he was willing to go ahead. He had a cancellation which Luciano could have if he decided immediately. He would be admitted tomorrow for pre-operative tests and preparation and Luciano would perform the operation the day after.

Vittorio's phone was ringing. *'Pronto! Vittorio… Si, Lucy?'*

He felt a shiver of excitement at the sound of her voice. But at the same time he wished he could confide in her about what was happening to him.

'Are you coming to Pronto Soccorso this morning, Vittorio?'

Vittorio smiled. He loved the way Lucy's voice lilted when she was speaking Italian. Her accent was improving all the time but he hoped she wouldn't lose the charming English overtones that still lingered there. Especially when she became excited.

'Of course I'm coming in. Is there a problem?'

'I just wondered when you were coming in, that's all,' Lucy said, lowering her voice and changing to English as one of the nurses passed by. 'I'm taking a quick break in Sister's office before I go back to work.'

'I'll join you as soon as I've finished off here.'

Vittorio heard the click of the phone at the other end. How would he survive for a whole week without her? And if he was worrying about a week's separation, what would it be like to never see her again?

Vittorio had no chance to talk to Lucy about personal matters whenever they were working together during the rest of the day. A pleasure boat had capsized on the river and survivors were being brought in as soon as he arrived in Pronto Soccorso. The paramedics had been brilliant at reviving the patients who'd been under water. But one victim hadn't responded. They'd used all the resuscitation techniques available but after half an hour of intensive work on their patient, Vittorio had to pronounce her dead.

Lucy pulled herself upright and turned away from the depressing scene. Dedicated doctors and nurses, looking dejected and weary, were having to finally admit defeat.

'There's nothing more we can do here, Lucy,' Vittorio said, as soon as he'd asked the nursing staff to finish off the necessary work. One of them was already wheeling in the trolley required after a death.

'I'll do the death certificate,' Vittorio continued. 'Do we have a name?'

The medical team assembled around the still figure glanced at each other. One of the paramedics who'd stayed with the resuscitation team said that the young lady had had no documentation on her. None of the other passengers knew who she was. She'd been by herself.

Lucy turned back to look down at the still figure. Their patient looked as if she was in her late teens or early twenties. Her long dark hair lay around her like a halo.

'She looks so peaceful,' one of the junior nurses said, as she began swabbing the pale, motionless face. 'I didn't know dead people could look so beautiful.'

Lucy swallowed hard as she turned away. 'I've got another patient waiting for me,' she told Vittorio quickly.

'So have I.'

They went out of the treatment room and crossed the assessment area together.

'Are you free this evening, Lucy?' Vittorio said, quietly in English.

She smiled. 'I could be.'

The thought of an evening with Vittorio was just what

she needed to take her mind off the gruelling session she'd just undertaken.

'You're going to be in Milano for a week?' Lucy said.

They were sitting on the sofa in Vittorio's living room as he made his announcement. He'd uncorked the wine in the kitchen and had brought the bottle and two glasses through. He thought he'd chosen the right moment. Lucy was sipping her wine and beginning to relax after the busy day they'd had. If he could have put it off any longer he would have done. He prayed that it wasn't going to spoil their evening.

Lucy put down her glass. 'When are you going?'

'Tomorrow.'

'Tomorrow?'

'There's a family health problem.'

Even to his own ears it sounded too vague an answer. It was one thing to use obscure phrases when applying for leave of absence but quite another to face someone you were close to.

'Oh, I'm so sorry,' Lucy said.

That made Vittorio feel even worse. 'It's...it's not serious...but serious enough for me to have to go to Milano for a week. Now—'

'Which member of the family is it?'

'My grandmother is ill. Cardiac problems.'

Vittorio's answer came out as if he'd rehearsed it. It was perfectly true that his grandmother was ill with cardiac problems. She'd been ill for a number of years now and had confounded doctors time and time again by rallying round and surviving. But at the moment there was no reason to believe that she wouldn't survive for some time to come.

Vittorio took a deep breath. He hated being economical with the truth. He'd always been a rotten liar! He wished he didn't have to do this. He'd never been any good at deception. It made him feel so awful. But this was only a little white lie he was telling.

'When did you know you would have to go to Milano?'

'Not until this morning.'

That at least was true!

'I'd hoped I'd be granted leave of absence but I had to check on the possibility with Carlos. He's agreed to cover for me during the week I'll be away.'

'I see.'

Lucy knew she didn't really see what was going on. Why did she feel there was something strange about the situation? She'd spoken to Carlos that morning but he hadn't mentioned anything about the arrangements he'd made with Vittorio. He'd seemed in a great hurry to get away from her.

'So Carlos is taking over from you tomorrow morning?'

'Yes. I have an early start.' Vittorio put his arm around Lucy and drew her into the circle of his embrace. He lowered his head and kissed her gently.

She responded immediately, clinging to him as if she was afraid the kiss wouldn't last. He caressed her tenderly, oh, so tenderly, teasing the soft skin beneath her blouse as she arched against him.

'I want to make love to you,' he whispered huskily. 'It's going to be agony without you for a whole week.'

'Mmm…' Lucy entwined her arms around his neck.

As he swept her up into his arms and carried her through to the bedroom, he couldn't help remembering that Luciano had told him he would have to abstain from love-making for some time after the operation. He'd said he couldn't specify how long until after the surgery. Vittorio groaned inwardly as he thought how difficult it would be to keep to the post-operative instructions when he was reunited with Lucy.

'What are you thinking about, Vittorio?' Lucy asked as she snuggled against him.

'I'm thinking just how much I'm going to miss you,' he whispered as he held her close against him.

He caressed her tenderly, but there was a poignancy about their love-making this evening. It was impossible for either of them to forget that they would have to be apart for a whole week.

Vittorio found himself wanting to remember these precious moments in the days to come. He wanted to keep Lucy enshrined in his heart until they met again.

Lucy was holding herself close against him, murmuring, now moaning, and finally calling out his name as she climaxed time after time…

Afterwards they lay very still, locked in each other's arms, neither of them wanting to think about the morning.

'How long have we got?' Lucy asked as she watched the dawn light creeping over the windowsill.

She'd slept fitfully after they'd made love but now she was ready to face the day.

'Long enough,' Vittorio murmured sleepily as he reached for her.

This time when they made love it was slow, lingering, both of them trying to make the heavenly experience last as long as they could…

Lucy swung her legs over the side of the bed and stood up, determinedly. If she stayed any longer in Vittorio's bed they would make love again and she would feel even more depressed than she did now. As they'd made love just now she'd been unable to forget that this was the last time she would be with Vittorio for a week. Their first separation since the beginning of their affair.

Vittorio put out his hand. 'Don't go yet, Lucy. Stay.'

She gave him a sad smile. 'Stay and prolong the farewells.' She took a deep breath. 'It's only a week, Vittorio,' she said briskly. 'It will soon pass. We'll both be very busy.'

She padded on bare feet towards the living room, picking up her strewn garments as she went. Vittorio followed her. Lucy pulled on her blouse and skirt, bundling the rest of her things under her arm.

'I've only got to go down the corridor. Don't try to stop me, Vittorio. I'll see you next week. I'll phone you on your mobile. Will you phone me?'

Vittorio felt a moment of panic. Of course there would have to be phone calls between them! But what if Lucy phoned him on his mobile when he was under the anaesthetic? He would have to make contingency plans with Luciano. Put him in charge of his mobile or something.

'Of course I'll phone you,' he said.

Lucy paused at the door as Vittorio took her in his arms. His kiss was tender, poignant, touchingly loving before he released her from his arms, holding open the door as he watched her walk away down the dimly lit, deserted corridor.

Then he went back to his lonely bed, lying back on the pillows, one hand under his head as he contemplated the week ahead. Everything had moved so quickly. There was no turning back. It would have been much easier for him if he'd confided in Lucy. But he knew he couldn't do that. It had to remain secret, along with the other details he'd withheld about his former life.

He closed his eyes as he tried to convince himself he was taking the right course of action. As soon as he knew the outcome of his operation he would know what he had to do next...wouldn't he?

He shivered as he thought how impossibly dejected he would feel if the operation was unsuccessful...especially now that he had half decided to take the plunge and try to move on to a more permanent relationship with Lucy.

All supposing she was in agreement which, given her past suffering, was proving difficult to predict...

CHAPTER SEVEN

'IT'S seemed such a long week since Vittorio went to Milan!' Lucy told Sarah as they sat in the elegant drawing room of the Rome apartment. 'If we hadn't been so busy in Accident and Emergency I would have found it even longer. Thank goodness he's due back tomorrow.'

Sarah put down her delicate porcelain teacup on its saucer and faced her sister. 'I'm glad you've told me all about your feelings for Vittorio, Lucy. You know, for the past couple of years I've felt we were drifting apart. We didn't have that close bond we had when we were kids, did we?'

Lucy helped herself to another of the delicious biscuits her sister had baked that morning. 'We've both been a bit too secretive with each other, haven't we?'

'Especially you, Lucy!'

Lucy looked across the highly polished antique Italian coffee-table towards her twin. 'Have I been any more secretive than you?'

'Well, I'd no idea you were having a relationship with...what was he called?'

'You mean Bluebeard?' Lucy suggested facetiously.

The two sisters giggled and Lucy started choking on her biscuit. She picked up her cup of tea and swallowed a large gulp.

'That's better! Do you know, Sarah,' Lucy continued as soon as she'd managed to speak again, 'that's the first time I've been able to see the funny side of my awful affair with Mark. I mean, it could have been a lot worse, couldn't it?'

'As we used to say when we were younger, you could have been raped, pillaged, murdered in your bed…'

They were both laughing again. 'Oh Lucy, it's so good to have a heart to heart with you,' Sarah said.

'Talking of heart to hearts, why didn't you let me know you were pregnant as soon as you found out, Sarah?'

'Honestly, Lucy, it was all so difficult! Can you imagine how I felt when I was starting a new job here, discovering I was unintentionally pregnant by Robin. Robin and I had agreed to separate before I knew I was pregnant, so I had to dutifully let him know he was going to be a father and hope he wouldn't want to be too much involved.'

'And then along came Carlos,' Lucy said. 'What was it like, falling in love when you were pregnant?'

Sarah smiled. 'Heavenly! We had a lot of problems to resolve but, looking back now, I realise just how happy I was even with all the problems.'

'I wish you'd told me more about it at the time, Sarah. Let's not keep secrets from each other again. Let's tell each other everything like we always did when we were kids. Talking of which—secrets, that is—has Carlos told you anything about the supposed family health problem that's the reason for Vittorio taking a week's leave of absence?'

'Why do you say supposed family health problem?' Sarah asked.

Lucy hesitated. 'Well, it all seems a bit unlikely to me. Before Vittorio announced he was going off to Milan for a week he'd never mentioned anything about family health problems. He's so secretive. I can't help worrying that he might have some kind of mistress in Milano…just as Mark did…except Mark had a wife. It's a case of once bitten, twice shy with me. I'm always suspicious now.'

'Lucy, you mustn't think like that! Vittorio is besotted with you. Carlos says so. That's all he's told me. Whenever I ask him why he thinks so, he goes all quiet and says he can't divulge a confidence.'

Lucy nodded. 'Tell me about it! Do you think all Italian men are like that? Vittorio has told me so little about the tragic circumstances of his wife's death. Do you know anything?'

Sarah shook her head. 'I think Carlos knows some of the details but I'm sure he feels he's not at liberty to tell me. He did once start to tell me that Vittorio feels guilty about the way his wife died, but as soon as he'd said it he told me to forget what he'd said.'

Lucy frowned. 'Did you know he had a baby son who died?'

'How awful! No, I didn't know that. Poor Vittorio. No wonder he seemed such an enigma when he first arrived here in Rome. You've certainly helped to bring him out of his shell.'

'I wish! I bring him out for a while, ask him a few questions and then he clams up on me.'

'Give him time, Lucy. Don't worry about what he's doing in Milan. I'm sure it's a genuine family health problem if Carlos is backing his story.'

Lucy remained thoughtful. 'I wish I could be as sure as you are. I'll be so relieved when he returns. He seemed very uneasy when he was talking about going to Milan. He said his grandmother was ill, but it didn't sound convincing to me. I have a feeling he might have given the real reason to Carlos. But whenever I've seen

Carlos at work, he's been equally unforthcoming. So, putting two and two together...'

'You're making five, Lucy! Vittorio's grandmother is ill, that's all. Carlos wouldn't have agreed to taking Vittorio's place if he thought—'

'I think they're in league with each other,' Lucy said, leaning forward towards her sister.

'Possibly. But that doesn't mean Vittorio is being unfaithful to you.'

'Sarah, we're not in any way bound to each other. We both agreed that all we wanted was a light romance and that anything else—'

'Rubbish! Don't give me that fairy story, Lucy. You're both madly in love. I've seen you together. My feeling is that before very long Vittorio will propose something more permanent. I think you've helped him get over his difficult loss and he's ready to move on. If he asked you to marry him, would you—?'

'Oh, Sarah, for heaven's sake! Stop jumping the gun! Nothing is further from—'

'But if he did ask you, what would you say?'

Lucy closed her eyes. 'Since the miscarriage I've always said I didn't intend to marry or have children. But if I'm honest, I would...I would say yes.'

'I thought so. So don't you think it's time you got yourself prepared for such an eventuality? Don't you think it's time you took those fertility tests you should have taken after your miscarriage?'

'Honestly, Sarah, only a twin sister could be as brutally honest as you are!'

'Somebody's got to tell you! You know damn well you'll want kids if a marriage is on the cards!'

'A marriage isn't on the cards. Well, not mine anyway. Yours is all planned but as for mine...Sarah, I'm so scared that Vittorio will break my heart just as Mark did. Vittorio has taken off and left me without a good reason, just as Mark used to do. I don't think I can go through all that anguish again.'

'No, I'm sure you can't,' Sarah said slowly. 'But I still think you should get yourself checked out by a good gynaecologist. It can't do any harm and it will give you peace of mind.'

'OK, I will! But if I'm wrong about what Vittorio is up to this week...'

'You'll have lost nothing, Lucy. I know an excellent gynaecologist, a friend of Carlos who came to the apartment last week for a dinner party. Let me make an appointment for you. He has his own private clinic and isn't remotely involved with the Ospedale Tevere, so you needn't worry that someone will hear about it.'

Lucy leaned back against the cushions of the elegant sofa, glad that Sarah had stopped haranguing her. She knew her sister meant well but it was emotionally exhausting to explain how she felt. 'You're becoming very grand, Sarah.'

'In what way?'

'Well, dinner parties with distinguished consultants, living in this expensive apartment in the middle of Rome...'

'Oh, Lucy, don't be silly! I told you, Carlos's mother gave this apartment to us. Do you remember how we used to come here when we were children?'

'I used to be scared of spilling my fruit juice on this posh antique carpet, didn't you?'

'I once did!' Sarah said.

'I remember. Mum was mortified that you'd shown her up in front of the dauntingly elegant Signorina Vincenzi. Trust you, Sarah! You always were a scalliwag!'

'And you were always regarded as the sensible one, Lucy.'

'Not any more! I feel terribly vulnerable at the moment.'

'You'll come through,' Sarah said. 'Carlos and I had a difficult time but everything worked out for the best.'

Lucy sighed. 'You seem to have everything sorted now. When is Charlotte going to be allowed out of hospital?'

'Next week. She's only a month old now and she was two months premature. I go to see her every day in hospital but it's not the same as looking after her myself. When did you last see Charlotte, Lucy?'

Lucy smiled. 'This morning. I go to see her every day, Sarah. I'm very proud of my beautiful little niece.'

She stood up. 'I've got to get back. I did a split duty today so that I could come and have a long chat with you. Thanks for helping me, Sarah.'

Sarah hugged her sister. 'I hope I have been able to help. You helped me when I eventually told you about my pregnancy and everything that followed on from that.'

'Did I? I'm glad about that.' Lucy hesitated. 'I remember you told me that Carlos wants to adopt Charlotte.'

Sarah smiled. 'The documentation is all going through. The adoption should be complete in time for our wedding. You have put the wedding date down in your diary haven't you, Lucy?'

'Of course. I was talking to Mum the other night on the phone and every other sentence was about her plans for the wedding in our village. Apparently she's inviting the world and his wife.'

'Shall I give Mum Vittorio's name, and ask her to invite him, Lucy? Carlos thinks I should.'

'Definitely not!' Lucy drew in her breath. 'Our relationship is still very...well, unsettled, for want of a better word.'

'You make it sound like the weather.' Sarah giggled. 'Sunny in parts and—'

'And unresolved clouds hovering overhead,' Lucy finished off. 'It could improve but—'

'You mean the outlook will be much brighter. Always look on the bright side, Lucy.'

Sarah walked to the door with Lucy. The two sisters hugged each other again.

'I'll be in touch about your appointment with my gynaecologist friend,' Sarah said.

'Thanks.'

As Lucy began to walk away across the thick pile carpet towards the lift she told herself that she would have to go ahead with it now. Sarah wouldn't let her duck out of it!

'Vittorio!' Lucy stared up from the patient she was examining. 'I wasn't expecting you back this afternoon. You said you might not be back until this evening.'

'My grandmother has made an excellent recovery,' Vittorio said quickly, 'so I thought I would come and see if everything is running smoothly in my department.'

He reached out to touch her hands. Oh, how he'd missed her! How he'd longed to hold her every night he'd been away. Even the night when he'd felt really groggy after the general anaesthetic.

Lucy felt a shiver of excitement as their hands touched but she held onto her emotions. Glancing down at the patient, she knew she had to remain professional.

'I'm just about to do a lumbar puncture Vittorio.'

'Need any help?'

'No, I've got an efficient nurse to assist me. You're probably tired after your journey from Milan.'

Looking at Vittorio, she could see that he looked visibly thinner, paler, as if he'd spent the whole week cooped up in a hospital somewhere. Well, it was only a theory but somehow she thought it was a possibility. If Vittorio really had undergone an operation, it was best he should rest.

'I'll go back to my room and unpack,' Vittorio said.

'Would you like to come round this evening, Vittorio?'

They were both very much aware that the young nurse was listening in. Even though they were speaking English, it was obviously a personal conversation.

'Yes, of course,' Vittorio said evenly, as he thought how difficult it was going to be to keep on an even keel this evening.

Even though his lower abdomen was still distinctly tender and painful from the operation performed by Luciano he knew he would still feel the same urge to hold Lucy in his arms and make love to her. But he mustn't! He'd promised Luciano not to undo his surgical expertise. Not for at least two weeks. However was he going to contain himself? And whatever was Lucy going to think when he displayed all the signs that he'd picked up a severe case of male frigidity?

'Good! I'm glad you're free tonight,' Lucy said lightly, as she turned back to check on her patient.

The nurse was positioning the trolley of instruments near the examination couch. Lucy selected a sterilised trocar and cannula. She'd already applied the local anaesthetic to the patient's spine so there would be no pain as she performed the lumbar puncture.

Paulo, her patient, was a twenty-two-year-old English-language student who'd been brought in by ambulance. He'd collapsed at the university during a lecture, complaining of excruciating headaches which had been getting worse over the last couple of weeks. Initial X-ray and MRI scans had revealed no abnormality in the skull and brain, so Lucy was now going to have the cerebrospinal fluid tested to see if there was any infection there.

Putting on sterile gloves, Lucy ran her fingers down Paulo's spine, selecting the space between the third and fourth lumbar vertibrae. Fixing the trocar in position, she inserted the cannula.

The patient, lying on his side with his knees drawn up in front of him, asked Lucy if she'd started work on his back yet.

Lucy smiled. 'I've just finished. Just got to put the cerebrospinal fluid in a test tube so the laboratory can do some more tests.'

'I didn't feel a thing! Thanks, Doctor.'

They were speaking English because Paulo said he needed the practice before his next exam and Lucy was always more than happy to speak English. She put the cerebrospinal fluid into a test tube and noted that the fluid appeared clear, with no blood clouding it.

She asked the nurse to take the sample along and request that it be dealt with as soon as possible.

'You can sit up now, Paulo.'

Lucy put some pillows behind the young man's head before sitting down on a chair at the side of the examination couch.

'Tell me about these headaches you've been having, Paulo.'

Her patient frowned. 'They've been getting steadily worse for the last two weeks. I keep thinking I've got a brain tumour.'

'Well, the good news is that the X-rays and MRI scans of your skull didn't detect any abnormality. There are other possibilities we will have to investigate.' She hesitated. 'But, tell me, why did you initially think it might be a brain tumour?'

Paulo frowned. 'My father died of a brain tumour when he was twenty-seven,' he said, his voice hoarse with emotion. 'I don't remember him. I got married last year and my wife is soon to have our baby. I hope I'll be around to see him grow up.'

'I'm sorry about your father. I can see why you might be worried.'

'Well, I'm twenty-two now. I keep wondering how long I've got.'

Lucy watched her patient's expression as he talked. He was a very intense young man, exceptionally bright, and as he'd told her earlier, ambitious.

'You've got a lot of worries at the moment,' she began carefully. 'Your final exams in linguistics, your first baby and—'

'Don't say it's all in the mind, Doctor! Believe me, these headaches are very real, I assure you.'

'I do believe you. Nobody's doubting the physical symptoms,' Lucy said quietly. 'I'm going to have you admitted for a few days' observation while we perform several other tests on you. You've no other obvious symptoms of disease, fortunately.'

'OK, there are no physical signs of abnormality, Doctor. But what about inherited susceptibility to a particular problem? Don't you think that a man with a father who died of a brain tumour has more than a chance of following in his footsteps?'

'Not necessarily,' Lucy replied carefully. 'Current research shows that there are many more factors than genetics which decide who will have a brain tumour and who won't. On the results of the tests so far I can be ninety-nine percent sure you will be one of the lucky ones.'

Paulo smiled. 'That's good news. But if you can't find any physical cause for my headaches…what then?'

'If the tests point to the fact that there is nothing physically wrong with you, Paulo, we'll have to suggest a change in lifestyle. Many severe headaches are brought on by stress. And I would say you've probably got a lot of that in your life at the moment.'

'I probably have,' Paulo said quietly. 'I've not had time to think about it for a long time. I feel under pressure all the time and so I just get on with the next task that presents itself in the hope I'll find some time to relax later. But that never seems to happen.'

'Maybe you should reconsider what's important in your life. Cut out any unnecessary commitments. Don't take on extra work at the university unless you have to, delegate to anybody who offers to help you wherever you can, that sort of thing.'

Paulo appeared to be thinking hard. 'I was thinking about signing up for another language class. I've always wanted to learn Spanish.'

'My advice is don't! Well, not at the moment anyway. You speak English and German as well as your native Italian, of course. You'll need time to be with your wife and child so don't tie yourself up any more than you need to.'

Paulo nodded. 'You know, Doctor, it's good to take

time out, isn't it? Just lying here now knowing that somebody is taking care of my problems has been relaxing in itself.'

'Good!' Lucy stood up. 'I'll see you settled into the primary care unit and then I'll have to leave you.'

'It's so good to be back,' Vittorio said, as he stretched out his legs in front of him. They were sitting on the sofa in Lucy's room that evening, discussing the week they'd spent apart. Vittorio was trying not to appear edgy, but some of Lucy's questions were a bit difficult to answer truthfully.

'As I told you, my grandmother has made a remarkable recovery,' Vittorio said in answer to Lucy's most recent question.

'Is she out of hospital?'

'Hospital? Oh, yes, she's at home.'

'I could tell you were in a hospital when I phoned you the day after you arrived, at the beginning of the week,' Lucy said quietly. 'The background noise of a hospital is unmistakable, isn't it?'

Vittorio looked across at Lucy questioningly. It was almost as if she was trying to trip him up! He remembered the phone call she'd made when he'd been coming round from the anaesthetic. Luciano had handed him his mobile when he'd groggily insisted that he was feeling up to answering a call from Lucy.

'I heard you talking to someone called Luciano. Is he a doctor at the hospital where...?'

'What is this?' Vittorio said testily. 'Why are you quizzing me like this? Do I have to account for every moment of my time away from here?'

'I'm sure I don't know what you mean,' Lucy said, trying desperately to remain cool.

She stood up. 'Would you like a glass of wine, Vittorio? That would help to relax you after—'

'I'm perfectly relaxed!' Vittorio was almost shouting with frustration. Some homecoming! He was beside himself with sexual frustration! He longed to take Lucy in his arms and here she was asking all these questions!

He glared at her. 'You're behaving like a suspicious detective. What is this? The Spanish Inquisition?'

He took a deep breath as he told himself it was only his conscience that was troubling him. He would love to tell Lucy the truth but that wasn't possible.

'Perhaps I'll have that glass of wine now,' he said, standing up and moving towards her. 'I'll open the bottle in a moment, but first I need to hold you.'

As he took her in his arms he could feel her melting against him. It was going to be so hard to follow Luciano's instructions. *No love-making for at least a couple of weeks! Return for a check-up when all the internal sutures have been completely absorbed in six or seven weeks.*

'I've missed you so much,' he whispered.

'Me too.' But as she said it, she could feel the anxiety creeping up inside her. She didn't believe his story about family problems. She couldn't bear to be deceived by a man she loved twice in her life. If she couldn't trust Vittorio then she had to end their relationship before she became too involved.

There and then, she decided she wouldn't ask Carlos to renew her contract when it expired in October. It was no use putting herself through any more emotional trauma.

Completely unaware of Lucy's decision, Vittorio moved away to bring the bottle of wine in from the kitchen. He uncorked it and handed her a glass. They intertwined their hands as they raised their glasses towards each other's lips.

'To health and happiness,' Vittorio said huskily as he drank from Lucy's glass.

'To health and happiness,' Lucy repeated as convincingly as she could.

But as she drank from Vittorio's glass she was full of apprehension about the future. It wasn't going to be easy to stick to her resolutions. But for the sake of her future peace of mind she had to stand firm. Move on and pick up her life again...without Vittorio.

CHAPTER EIGHT

Lucy had been impressed with the décor of the gynaecological clinic when she'd arrived here for her first visit
two weeks ago. Now, as she waited for Giorgio Mantelli,
the gynaecologist who'd been in charge of the fertility
investigations she'd undergone, she tried to focus her
mind on the pleasing pastel shades of the curtains that
looked out onto a soothingly peaceful garden.

She looked down at the thick cream-coloured carpet
beneath her feet. She'd actually been out and bought a
pair of fabulous Italian leather shoes yesterday in a shop
that Sarah had taken her to. It had been near to the
Spanish Steps and the two of them had lunched in a
restaurant nearby after they'd spent far more on shoes
than either of them had ever contemplated.

If it hadn't been for Sarah she probably wouldn't have
gone ahead with these fertility tests in the first place.
Sarah had insisted that the appointment be made.
Insisted that Lucy go through with it. Insisted that she
should take it as a routine appointment with a gynaecologist that should have been made after her miscarriage. Even though the idea of having a child with
Vittorio was totally improbable now.

Or was it? Again, glancing around at her luxurious
surroundings, Lucy could feel herself wavering. The joy
of having a baby with Vittorio would be endless. Except
she wasn't sure she could trust him any more than she
should have trusted Mark. And even if she could, she
knew that Vittorio wouldn't dare to commit himself to

having a family again. He was too badly scarred by the trauma of losing his wife and child.

She still didn't know the full extent of that trauma, but it had obviously changed him for life so she mustn't even allow herself to dream about loving Vittorio in a permanent way, let alone have his babies. She tried to convince herself that she was simply having the gynaecological check she should have had a long time ago.

'You need something to keep your mind off worrying about the tests you've undergone,' Sarah had told her on a recent shopping day out, as they'd drunk campari and soda aperitifs whilst studying the lunch menu.

That was certainly true! During the last two weeks, she'd worried constantly that her miscarriage might have damaged her internal organs.

'And you a doctor!' Sarah had said. 'Actually, I'm just as bad. Take great care with my patients but never find time for myself. Well, now's the time to start thinking about yourself, Lucy.'

Now, as she sipped the coffee that the nurse had brought her while she waited for Giorgio Mantelli, she remembered how surprised the gynaecologist had looked at her cavalier attitude to the post-operative situation following her miscarriage. She'd tried to explain that she'd been in a state of shock, that she hadn't wanted to dwell on what had been happening to her. It had all been so closely associated with the man who'd devastated her life and she'd wanted to forget the whole episode.

As the memories flooded back, she wished she'd talked to Sarah about it at the time. Sarah would have been able to make an objective judgement on what she should have done without her reaction being coloured by anger at the man who'd caused her to suffer.

Well, today was the day that she was going to hear

the results of her tests and there was nothing more she could do but wait. She realised that during the last two weeks, since Vittorio had come back from his mysterious visit to Milan, their relationship had changed in some indefinable way.

They'd enjoyed going out together as they always had. It was so wonderful to be living in Rome, able to visit the famous historic sights, go to the theatre, wander in the beautiful parks, sample the excellent cuisine that was on offer in even the smallest restaurant. But when they'd been totally alone, away from the crowds, Vittorio had seemed to be holding himself in check.

Oh, he'd been infinitely tender with her as he always had been. They'd embraced, held each other closely, kissed each other gently. But all the time Vittorio had made it quite plain that he didn't want to become too sexually involved.

Which was making her more and more suspicious of his reason for going to Milan. What if the sick grandmother had really been a vibrant mistress?

The thought haunted her continually and she knew she couldn't bear the anguish if she was proved right. She couldn't go through what she'd gone through with Mark so it was best that she should be prepared for the end of their affair. It had been wonderful while it had lasted, but she must try to keep something back for the time when she would return to England and pick up her life again where she'd left off before Vittorio had swept her off her feet.

'Good morning, Lucy,' Giorgio said as he came in, a beaming smile on his large, good-natured face.

'Good morning, Giorgio,' Lucy replied as she put down her coffee-cup on the table beside her comfortable armchair.

She smiled up at the gynaecologist. He was an affable man who loved to speak English. Lucy thought his English was excellent. When he spoke there were slight overtones of an American accent. At her first appointment Giorgio had told her that he'd spent several years working in America. He'd added, with a twinkle in his eye, that he still liked to watch American films whenever he could.

Giorgio sat down in the armchair opposite Lucy. Since she'd first arrived here she'd struck up a good rapport with this genial, middle aged family man. She'd noticed that he always made a point of trying to put her at her ease so that she could say absolutely anything to him. And she usually did! She'd told him all her secrets without any embarrassment. That's what made a good gynaecologist. Someone a girl could really trust.

As she looked across the immaculate cream carpet towards him, she remembered how she'd spilled out her heart concerning the disastrous affair with Mark, her longing for the child she'd been carrying, her agony when she'd found she'd been having a miscarriage. She'd said that it was improbable that she would have a child with her current partner but had begun to think that at some point in the future she might like to have a child.

Giorgio had always listened, never passed judgement on anything she said, never suggested that she should have taken more care of her health after the miscarriage.

But what was done was done! She couldn't turn the clock back. And she was about to find out if her disastrous past was going to impinge on the future.

'I've got the results of all your tests here, Lucy,' Giorgio said, opening the large file in front of him. 'Most of them seem fine.'

Lucy found she was holding her breath. Most of them!

What about the minority that weren't? It was a bit like getting the end-of-term exam results except there was a lot more at stake here. Her whole future…

'I've got the results of your hysterosalpingosonogram. Let's just call it HSG for short.' Giorgio looked up and smiled encouragingly across at Lucy.

'That was the one where a little dye was placed into my uterus and an ultrasound scan was done, wasn't it?'

Giorgio nodded. 'As I told you at the time, many gynaecologists think the need for this test has been replaced by laparoscopy. But I firmly believe it is extremely accurate in determining the health—or otherwise—of the uterus and the Fallopian tubes.'

Lucy leaned forward attentively. Please, don't say you've found something wrong, she prayed silently.

'As you know, the uterus and tubes are particularly susceptible to infection immediately after a pregnancy has ended in a miscarriage and especially if a D and C has been necessary to remove all the tissue left behind by the foetus.'

'As in my case,' Lucy said quietly, almost under her breath.

'Yes.' The consultant paused and his expression became unnervingly sympathetic. 'Unfortunately…'

Giorgio cleared his throat before starting again.

No, oh, please, no, don't say it! Lucy clasped her hands tightly to disguise the fact that she was shaking with apprehension as she listened.

'Unfortunately, your uterus and tubes must have been subjected to some infection and inflammation in the post-operative stage. The Fallopian tube on your right side is blocked. The scarring is very advanced and therefore inoperable.'

He paused. 'Are you all right, Lucy?'

'Yes, I think so,' she said, shakily as she tried to make sense of what she'd just heard.

It was so strange being a patient. She understood exactly what Giorgio was saying but in her position as a patient she felt she had to clarify everything.

'Giorgio, you said that one of my tubes was irreparably damaged. That means that I can't ovulate on that side, doesn't it?'

Giorgio nodded. 'Exactly.'

'But how about the tube on the other side? Is that viable?'

'The tube on your left side has been scarred but it's not blocked. It appears to be fairly healthy.'

'It's possible to conceive with just one tube, isn't it, Giorgio?' she said, desperately clutching at straws. 'I've known patients with one tube blocked who managed to become pregnant.'

'You're quite right, Lucy. Let's hope you will be one of the lucky ones.'

'What do you rate my chances?'

Giorgio drew in his breath, studying the tips of his fingers as he frowned. 'I'm not a gambling man. I don't like to make predictions of this nature. Each patient is different, as you know. Only time will tell what the future holds. Now, let's look at the results of the other tests, shall we?'

Lucy listened as if in a trance to the sound of Giorgio's voice. He'd given her the bad news first and now seemed anxious to make amends as it were, by telling her about her general health. Everything was excellent. She was in fine physical shape for a woman of thirty.

Thirty. The age she'd dreaded whenever she'd thought

about it in her twenties. But she was in excellent health in every way except the department she wanted to be perfect in.

'So how was your shopping expedition with Sarah?' Vittorio asked as he opened the door to his room that evening.

'Oh, we didn't buy much today.'

Lucy sank down on the sofa, suddenly feeling desperately tired. She'd had to tell another little white lie in order to explain where she was going on her day off.

'You seem to be doing an awful lot of shopping at the moment,' Vittorio said, as he handed her a glass of wine.

'Sarah needed some things for Charlotte. And I got some shoes.'

The more fabrications she invented the easier it seemed to be. Was this how the men in her life had managed to deceive her so easily? She squirmed inwardly at the implications.

'More shoes! You'll need a larger room to keep them all in soon.'

Lucy took a sip of her wine and leaned back against the cushions, breathing deeply to calm her nerves.

'Well, I've got to take advantage of my time here in Rome. My contract ends in October.'

Vittorio sank down on the sofa beside her. 'Lucy, you're going to renew your contract, aren't you?'

She hesitated. 'I'm not sure,' she said quietly, knowing full well that she'd intended to tell him the truth.

But what was the truth? That she planned to go back to England in October. Did she really think she could walk away from Vittorio and bear the pain of separation?

'You must renew your contract! You can't leave Rome now, not when—'

He broke off. He wanted so desperately to tell Lucy how he really felt about her. He stood up and walked over to the window, squeezing his fists tightly to prevent himself from blurting out the truth.

'What will you do if you don't renew your contract?' he asked evenly.

'I'll go back to England, probably into Accident and Emergency again.'

'But you haven't completely decided you're leaving Rome?'

He moved back across the room and drew her against him. This was what he'd feared. Losing the woman he loved. He hadn't meant to fall in love with Lucy. He'd tried so hard not to lose his heart again. But it had just happened, even though he'd tried so hard to remain emotionally detached.

She could feel her resolve melting away once more. The feel of Vittorio's arms around her was undermining her determination.

'No. I...I'm still thinking about it.'

Vittorio breathed a sigh of relief as he lowered his head, his lips gently teasing hers until his kiss deepened.

'Darling, you are so precious to me,' he whispered. 'When I'm holding you in my arms I don't mind about anything except the two of us.'

As she leaned against him, she could feel the dormant stirrings of passion deep down inside her.

He smiled down into her eyes, instinctively feeling her change of mood. He wanted so much to make love to her. He knew it would be safe now. The frustration of the past two weeks had been difficult to endure. Every time he'd been close to Lucy he'd longed to hold her more closely. But tonight...

He cupped her face with his hands, looking into her

eyes to gauge her reaction. 'I want so much to make love to you tonight, Lucy.'

She sighed as she clung to him. 'Mmm…'

Vittorio smiled as he scooped her up into his arms and carried her across to his bedroom.

As Lucy opened her eyes she could see the dark red light of the early morning sun creeping over the windowsill. It had been a hot night, so Vittorio had flung wide the windows at one point so they could both breathe in the cooling air. He'd held her close to him as they'd leaned out of the window, watching the comings and goings down on the forecourt of the hospital.

With Vittorio's arm encircling her waist, her body still tingling with the aftermath of their love-making, she'd felt strangely detached from the real world. She and Vittorio had been in their own private little heaven up here in his room.

Vittorio had drawn her back from the window. As he'd lifted her onto the bed beside him, she'd felt his body hardening again. As he'd begun to caress her again, oh, so tenderly she'd felt her own body responding and had moulded her body against his.

As she'd looked up into his eyes she'd wanted to drown herself in his tender, loving expression. She hoped to remember their love-making last night for the rest of her life, whatever happened in the future.

She gave a sigh of contentment as she remembered how she'd swooned into Vittorio's arms and been tantalised, caressed, led through into a heavenly world she hadn't known existed.

As his mouth closed over hers, she gave herself once more to the heavenly oblivion where there was no tomorrow, only today. She pressed herself against

Vittorio's virile, exciting body, revelling in the feel of his skin blending with hers, their sensations becoming more and more heightened as each one strove to merge into the furnace of their passion...

And when she climaxed again and again she cried out in a heavenly surge of exultation...

Coming down to earth was always difficult when she'd spent the whole night with Vittorio. As she made her way to the hospital that morning she tried very hard not to look like the cat that had got the cream. She was feeling so happy, so consumed by their passion that she found she was greeting everybody she met...in English!

Get a grip, girl, she told herself. No wonder she was getting strange looks. You're in Rome, remember? This is the Ospedale Tevere and they speak Italian here, so you'd better concentrate! And as she brought her mind back to the present situation, inevitably the doubts came flooding back.

But there was no use worrying now. She had a job to do. Only as she looked around the assessment area and began focusing her eyes on the patients waiting to be seen by a doctor did she really come down from cloud nine. Surprisingly and alarmingly, her first patient was little Niko, the seven-year-old who'd fractured his tibia and fibula in a fall from a wall last month. He'd been discharged from hospital soon after the operation to reduce the fractures in his leg.

He was lying very still on a trolley, his mother holding his hand.

'What happened to you, Niko?' Lucy asked gently, relieved to find that she could still speak Italian.

'My leg is very hot and painful,' Niko said despondently. 'Mama thinks it's poorly.'

When Niko had been first admitted, Lucy had found that Consuella, Niko's mother, was an extremely sensible and intelligent woman. The orthopaedic firm had had no hesitation in allowing the little boy home a few days after the operation to plate and screw the bones in his leg.

'I brought Niko back because I think something is bad inside his leg,' Niko's mother said, anxiously.

Lucy took the X-rays out of the packet and fixed them on the wall screen, switching on the background light.

'May I have a look, Lucy?' Consuella asked.

'Of course. This x-ray shows the original state of the two broken bones when Niko first came in. Because the tibia and fibula were broken in several places the surgeon had to put in these plates and screws to hold them in place.'

She turned back to examine her young patient. The orthopaedic technician had already removed the plaster that had been supporting his leg. Lucy could see at a glance that infection had set in. The red, swollen, malodorous skin around the wounds of the leg was indicative of an infection inside the tissues.

Lucy hoped the infection hadn't spread to the bones. If it was confined to the tissues it would be much easier to treat. She couldn't bear the thought that this dear little boy, of whom she'd grown very fond, might face possible amputation.

She needed expert advice on this case so she immediately paged Vittorio.

'You want me to have a look at Niko, I believe,' Vittorio said moments later as he came in through the cubicle door.

Lucy felt a sense of relief to be able to consult with an orthopaedic specialist.

'It looks as if we've got an infected leg here,' she said quietly.

Vittorio's expression became intensely serious as he examined Niko's leg.

'I'm going to arrange for you to come back into hospital, Niko,' Vittorio said, as he looked down at the little boy. 'We'll give you some special treatment to make you better again. Is that OK with you?'

Niko considered the question solemnly. 'Can I go in the ward with that big television? The one like a cinema screen?'

'I think that could be arranged for you, Niko,' Vittorio replied, with equal solemnity.

Lucy felt a surge of emotion as she watched the brilliant way that Vittorio had gained Niko's confidence. He was an absolute natural with children. He would be the most perfect father if…

'OK. I'll stay,' Niko conceded.

'Thank you, Niko,' Vittorio said. 'The nurses on that ward will be very pleased to see you again.'

He turned away. 'I've got to get a move on,' he told Lucy in English. 'Can you arrange everything for me with regard to Niko's treatment? Set up an IV with a continual flow of antibiotics. I'll write down my recommendations but you can use your own judgement on the actual antibiotic you use, of course. Something generic to start with, but make sure that after you've sent some tests to the lab you get the specific bug zapped on the head a.s.a.p.'

'Of course.'

'I was just going to Theatre when you paged me. The new orthopaedic consultant has asked me to help him with a complicated hip restructuring.'

Lucy nodded. 'Thanks for coming. I'll deal with everything. See you later, Vittorio.'

His serious expression changed as he touched her hand briefly. 'I certainly hope so. Tonight...?'

She smiled up into his eyes, trying to remain totally professional and failing hopelessly.

'I think I can make it,' she said softly.

During the next week, Lucy found she was constantly worrying about how long she should stay in Rome. Her work completely absorbed her when she was on duty, but off duty the thought was never far from her mind.

During the last few days, she'd spent as much time as she could spare with young Niko in the children's ward, checking on the administration of his intravenous antibiotics, making sure that all of Vittorio's recommendations on treatment were carried out and explaining to Niko and his devoted mother, Consuella, what was actually happening. Niko was becoming decidedly restless, having been lying still for most of the time, wired up to a drip.

As Lucy woke up on the day her period was due, she remembered that today was the day that Vittorio was going to operate on Niko. He'd advised the new orthopaedic consultant that he thought the plates and screws might be the source of infection and he would like to have them removed. Vittorio, as senior orthopaedic surgeon in the hospital, was immediately asked if he would agree to do the operation.

As so much was at stake, Vittorio had readily agreed. He knew that in order to hold the leg firmly in a position where the bones would heal, he would have to put steel rods through the bones and attach these to external fixators.

The operation was scheduled for that morning. Lucy had promised Niko she would call in on her way to Pronto Soccorso and stay for a few minutes. Last night when Lucy and Vittorio had been together they'd both discussed the day ahead and had agreed that for the sake of their precious little patient they should have an early night in their separate beds.

She began to quietly sing Mimi's song under her breath as she flung back the covers and prepared for her shower.

She felt so happy, remembering that night she and Vittorio had spent at the opera. As she started walking over towards her little shower room she remembered that Vittorio had said he'd got tickets for another opera evening soon.

She was looking forward to it. She was looking forward to all the time they were able to spend together. But she was aware that time was running out. That she had to come to a decision soon. To trust Vittorio completely and possibly have her heart broken again? Or to walk away from their affair and mend her already bruised heart?

Thank goodness she could lose herself in her work today!

'Hello, Niko,' Lucy said, as she smiled down at her little patient. 'Did you sleep well?'

As she listened to the small boy chattering she hoped that she was putting on a good performance at pretending all was well in her own life. Compared to Niko's problems she was the luckiest woman in the world so she'd better not start feeling sorry for herself!

Vittorio had told her that if the operation he was going

to perform today wasn't a success, there was a distinct possibility that he might have to amputate.

'They haven't let me watch that big television, Lucy,' Niko said. 'They wouldn't let me get out of bed.'

'Well, once you've got fixators in your leg you'll be able to get around on crutches,' Lucy said.

'Vittorio told me that fixators make you look like a soldier from the old days with armour on,' Niko said.

'You'll be very special with your fixators on.' Lucy looked around the ward. 'Look, Niko, nobody else has got fixators, have they?'

Niko smiled. 'I'll be sort of…well, king of the ward, won't I?'

'You certainly will.'

Lucy turned away as the ward sister arrived carrying a kidney dish holding Niko's pre-med.

'Sister is here to give you the injection you need before your operation. You'll start to feel a bit sleepy in a nice sort of way. Then when they take you to Theatre you'll have another injection and then you'll go to sleep.'

'OK.' Niko held out his arm. 'Let's get on with it, shall we?'

Lucy glanced down at Consuella who was sitting quietly in a chair at the side of her son's bed. She was clearly holding back the tears for the sake of her beloved son.

'Are you all right, Consuella?' Lucy whispered.

Consuella nodded. 'I'm going round to see my mother for a couple of hours when Niko goes into Theatre. I'll be back later.'

'So will I,' Lucy said. 'Niko is in good hands. Vittorio is a top-class orthopaedic surgeon.'

'I know,' Consuella said. 'He's also very kind. You're very lucky, Lucy.'

'Lucky?'

Consuella smiled. 'I can see that you two were made for each other. I've seen the way you look at each other. You ought to bottle that special feeling you have. You'd make a fortune.'

'I didn't know it showed.'

'Of course it shows. And, please, don't try to disguise it. I was in love like you are with Niko's father. He died of leukaemia. You have to take each day and live it to the full, Lucy. Nothing matters except your love for each other.'

'It's not as easy as you think, Consuella. But I'll try to remember what you said.'

As she turned her attention back to her little patient she was feeling even more confused by Consuella's words. Yes, it was wonderful to be in love. But often there was a heavy price to pay. If she felt she could trust Vittorio implicitly it might be worth risking. But as she felt at the moment, she knew it would be foolish to take a chance.

She put the thoughts from her mind as she bent down and stroked Niko's forehead. Her little patient was already closing his eyes drowsily. She would try not to worry about what he was going to undergo in theatre.

He would be safe with Vittorio. As for her own situation? She wished she could feel she would be safe with Vittorio...but she knew she would never be sure.

She must bring an end to their affair...and the sooner she could pluck up her courage the better...

CHAPTER NINE

THROUGHOUT the month of September Lucy found that Pronto Soccorso had never been busier. Tourists of every nationality were flocking to Rome. This was the best time of the year when the sun was still warm but not too hot. And more tourists, all in free and easy holiday mood, meant more casualties.

Vittorio had called in Carlos for a meeting and they had agreed that the department needed more staff. Three more doctors were recruited and another six nurses. This meant that the work load was more evenly shared out between the Accident and Emergency staff.

Carlos had told Vittorio that he intended to return in October as a senior consultant on the general surgical firm but Sarah hadn't yet decided when she was coming back.

Lucy went over to see her sister whenever she could. It was so good to see Sarah happily settled with the man she loved and the baby who was the centre of both their lives. One day when she was having a relaxing afternoon at the apartment, the baby asleep in her nursery, Lucy asked Sarah when she was going back to work at the hospital.

Sarah smiled. 'Honestly, Lucy, I really can't make up my mind. I'm supposed to be back in Pronto Soccorso by the middle of October, but I'm just enjoying being a full-time mum at the moment.'

'Are you going to keep your trained nurse on here when you go back to work?'

'Oh, I'll have to. Miranda is very experienced with premature babies. Charlotte was eight weeks premature so we can't take any chances. I have total faith in Miranda but Carlos thinks I should stay home for a while longer.'

'How are the wedding plans coming along?'

Sarah smiled. 'Mum has finally allowed me to have a say in some of the arrangements. We had a long phone call the other evening. Our village church is booked for the second week in October. Mum's organised the caterers for the reception which we'll hold on the big lawn—you know, overlooking the river. Somebody's going to erect a marquee and Dad has filled the cellar with cases of champagne—enough for the whole of Yorkshire, Mum said.'

Lucy smiled. 'Sounds like our parents are enjoying themselves.'

Sarah leaned towards her sister along the sofa. 'Well, I think Mum is getting a bit tired and when she's tired she gets nervous, doesn't she?'

Lucy nodded. 'Anything I can do to help her, do you think?'

Sarah hesitated. 'She did actually say she wished one of us could go home for the week before the wedding. Just to give her moral support, hold her hand when she gets weepy, that sort of thing...'

'Actually, I would go home if I could take a week off,' Lucy said carefully.

'Oh, I'm sure Carlos could arrange that,' Sarah said quickly. 'He's been taking on extra staff, hasn't he?'

'Yes, he has.'

Lucy poured herself another cup of tea and settled back against the comfy sofa cushions. She enjoyed having these heart-to-heart talks with her twin. It was like being at home again without the hassle of the air journey.

'Another cake, Lucy,' Sarah said, holding out the plate.

'I'd love one. You're a real earth mother nowadays, aren't you?'

Sarah smiled. 'It's all this maternal instinct that comes packaged in with the baby. Just wait until you…' Her voice trailed away.

'It's OK. As I told you, my fertility tests were rather inconclusive. But it's not as if I'm trying for a baby or anything so…'

'But some time in the future, when you and Vittorio have…'

'Sarah, I don't think Vittorio and I will be together much longer.'

'How can you say that? When the two of you are always together.'

'For my part, I'm simply making the most of what we've got and not looking too far ahead. But I feel that sooner or later Vittorio will break my heart just as easily as Mark did.'

'Vittorio isn't remotely like Mark!'

'Maybe not. But I can't help having doubts about a long-term relationship with him. That's why I think it would be a good idea if I took a week off and went home while I sort out my feelings about the future. While I'm helping Mum I'll be away from Vittorio and I'll be able to think objectively.'

Sarah hesitated. 'I think you're probably right to take time out away from Vittorio if you've got all these doubts.'

Lucy stood up. 'I've got to go back to hospital. I'll phone Mum tonight.'

Sarah stood up and hugged her sister. 'Mum will be so happy you're going. I'd go home myself but I don't think having a baby around the house in the week before the wedding is a good idea.'

On duty that evening Lucy was occupied most of the time with minor injuries. First there was a student who'd been hit with a broken bottle in a dispute at the university. Lucy inserted stitches in his face where there was a long cut. He was a handsome young man and worried that he would be scarred for life.

Lucy had to be extremely careful about how she replied to his questions. She had to be honest and say that there would be some scarring but that plastic surgery might be the answer later on.

The young man pulled a wry face. 'You mean when I've made my money as a good-looking actor! Not much chance of that now that I look like this! Although perhaps I could play the part of a monster!'

When Lucy left the young student to the ministrations of his anxious mother, she'd formed the opinion that he had enough resilience to take whatever life threw at him. And plastic surgery techniques were advancing all the time.

Following this there was a succession of cuts requiring sutures, bones needing X-ray before the appropriate treatment and a cardiac-arrest patient who was successfully revived.

So it was late in the evening before she was able to call in at the children's ward and see young Niko. The little boy's face lit up when he saw her. He was sitting on top of his bed, reading.

'So, how are you Niko?' Lucy said, sitting down on the chair at the side of his bed.

'I'm fine! I've been walking around the ward all day with my fixators on. My leg feels a bit heavy with all these spikes sticking out but I can manage with my crutches. Let me show you, Lucy!'

Niko swung both legs over the side of the bed, grabbed his crutches and proceeded to walk away down the ward at a quick pace.

'Excellent!' Lucy said when he came back, smiling happily all over his face.

'Vittorio says I can go home soon with my fixators on and keep coming back to Outpatients. He's not going to chop my leg off either.'

Lucy drew in her breath. 'I didn't think—'

'Oh, yes, Vittorio warned my mum before the operation that he might not be able to mend it. So it's great I've still got two legs, isn't it? I think I'd like to be a footballer when I grow up.'

'You've certainly got the courage for it, Niko.'

Lucy looked up as she saw Vittorio walking in through the ward door. He made a beeline towards her as she sat on top of the bed next to Niko. The three of them chatted for a few minutes before Vittorio said it was time he was going.

'So I suppose Lucy is going with you,' Niko said.

'Possibly,' Vittorio said quietly.

'My mum thinks you two look good together.'

'Does she?'

Listening to this exchange in Italian, Lucy found her cheeks were burning. Trust a child like Niko to be so forward and open!

As they walked off down the corridor together, neither of them spoke. It was as if the little boy's remarks had stunned them into silence.

Nearing Pronto Soccorso, Vittorio turned towards

Lucy. 'Will you come into my office for a moment? There's something we have to discuss as soon as possible and I don't want to do it out here in the corridor.'

Vittorio closed the door behind them. Lucy sank down into a comfortable chair near the window and Vittorio sat down nearby.

He leaned forward. 'Carlos tells me you're planning to go back to England.'

'I'm going to help my mother prepare for the wedding.'

'But you are coming back, aren't you?'

Lucy swallowed hard. She'd realised that it would be impossible to come to terms with her constant doubts. Maybe when she got back home in England her romance with Vittorio would all seem like a dream, something that she would be able to forget in time.

'As I said, at the end of the month I'm going back to England to help my mother prepare for Sarah's wedding. I'll have fulfilled my contractual obligations in covering for Sarah's maternity leave. By mid-October Sarah should have taken my place in Pronto Soccorso. If she decides not to return then another doctor will have to be appointed.'

'But that should be you, Lucy!'

'Not necessarily.'

Lucy felt suddenly calmer about the situation than she had done for weeks.

'You've thought everything through, haven't you?' Vittorio said evenly. 'Are you saying you're not going to come back to Rome?'

'I'm saying I haven't decided. Going home will give me the chance to think clearly.'

She hated herself for being so evasive about the situation, but she couldn't float along in their romantic illusion for much longer. She wasn't the sort of person who could continue in a situation of wait and see for the rest of her life. But she was going to make the most of the short time she had left here in Rome with Vittorio. The dream could go on…temporarily.

She reached up and touched the side of Vittorio's face, smoothing back the wrinkles that had appeared in his brow.

'It will all work out for the best,' she whispered as she reached up to kiss him tenderly on the lips.

He lowered his head so that their kiss could deepen. He held her against him, savouring the taste and the scent of her as their bodies began to mould together.

'Come back to my room,' he whispered. 'I want to make love to you all night long. You may be planning to leave me, but the romance hasn't ended yet, has it?'

Lucy smiled up into his eyes. 'Our romantic night is just beginning. So let's make the most of it…'

There was a poignancy about their love-making that night. Lucy clung to Vittorio, knowing that they might have very little time left together.

She knew it would be her own choice to end their affair, but it was a choice that had to be made. The love they'd shared was too precious to be spoilt by constantly being plagued by doubts.

She wasn't prepared to let that happen. Far better to end it sooner rather than later and live with her romantic memories rather than chase an impossible dream.

CHAPTER TEN

'OH, MUM, it's so good to be home again!' Lucy said as she poured her mother a cup of coffee from the cafetière.

They were sitting in the kitchen of the large old country house where Lucy had been born. The familiar smells…her mother's casserole in the oven being slowly cooked ready for the family lunch at midday, the scent of the polish from the wooden floor in the dining room adjacent to the kitchen, the lovely aroma of the roses from the garden that were still blooming at the beginning of October. All the nostalgia of her childhood was flooding back on her first morning back in the family fold.

'It's good to have you home, Lucy,' Jennifer Montgomery said, as she sipped her coffee. 'I told Sarah on the phone I needed some help but actually everything is already organised. I just wanted one of you to be here with me for these last few days before the wedding. Your father tries to be helpful but men don't actually understand about wedding nerves, do they? I mean, take Peggy Baxter's daughter's wedding last month for instance. Poor Peggy had been asking Charles for help for months but…'

Lucy didn't reply because she couldn't comment on men in general. She'd only had two men in her life who'd made an impact. The first one she wanted to forget, but Vittorio was completely unique. She would never forget Vittorio.

She was aware that her mother was still talking about

some wedding that didn't concern her. Her mother didn't really expect a reply. She was just happy to have her daughter listening with one ear. So long as Lucy gave assistance whenever it was needed, that would be fine.

'What I can't understand,' Jennifer was saying now, 'is why Carlos and Sarah can't have a proper honeymoon. Sarah says they're going straight back to Rome the day after the ceremony. They're going to go down to their house on the coast for a couple of days and then it's back to work at the hospital. I just think they're going to be so tired. And there's Charlotte to look after as well. I really think they should…'

In the days that followed her arrival in Yorkshire, Lucy found she was becoming more relaxed. She was as attentive as she could be with her parents, helping them out with the final preparations, answering the phone, checking that the marquee was going to arrive in time, speaking to the caterers and making sure that they would liaise with the florist about table decorations and place settings.

Concerned as she was that Sarah's wedding should be a success and that her mother would stay calm and not get too tired, Lucy found that Vittorio was constantly in her thoughts. They'd agreed not to contact each other. Lucy had said she wanted a complete break so that she could think about her future and Vittorio was respecting that.

But as she lay in bed one night, staring up at the alabaster cherubs on the ceiling of her childhood bedroom, she realised how much she missed Vittorio. But at the same time she was becoming more and more convinced that finishing their affair was the right course of action. If she didn't want to experience any more emotional agonising then she had to call a halt. And the sooner the better. No more procrastination! She had to let Vittorio know she wanted a clean break.

She would pick up her life where she'd left it three months ago. Reclaim her cottage at the other side of the village from the letting agency who'd been renting it out for Yorkshire Dales tourists on a weekly basis. It would be easy to get herself another post in Accident and Emergency at the hospital.

Yes, it would be hard making the break to begin with…trying to forget Vittorio. No, she would never be able to forget him. But soon the memories would fade…she hoped.

She stifled the sob that rose in her throat. It wouldn't be easy but that's what she had to do. She looked up at the cherubs on the ceiling again as she had so often done when she'd been a child and had felt confused about something. Especially during the teenage years when she'd been taking exams, going out with unsuitable boys—according to her mother! She could have sworn that one of the cherubs smiled at her.

Perhaps it was because she was planning a change of lifestyle. The cherubs had been there for her when she'd gone off to medical school. That had been a big wrench. But nothing could compare with the rift she was now planning!

Just thinking about Vittorio now made her miss him so much! It was affecting everything she did. And she'd been feeling decidedly under the weather for the last couple of days. Yesterday, she'd stayed in bed much longer than usual because she'd felt so tired and lethargic. Heaven knew why, because her quiet, domestic life here was so much easier than her frenetic days in Rome.

It was the travelling, the change in her diet, the change

in the rhythm of her life that was affecting her, she decided. Even her period was late and she was usually as regular as...

She drew in her breath, clamping a hand over her mouth to stifle the shriek that she'd almost made. Her missing period... Could it be possible that...? No! The consultant had given her such an unpromising report after he'd checked her out. Anyway, she was only firing on one Fallopian tube and that was a bit dodgy to say the least.

But from a medical point of view it wasn't totally impossible, was it? She put her hands over her abdomen just as she had done when she'd known she'd been carrying her last baby. Could a miracle have happened? Could she be carrying Vittorio's baby?

She swallowed hard. The implications were enormous. She was completely unprepared. It would be just like last time. An unplanned pregnancy. A mysteriously secretive partner...

What should she do if she really was pregnant?

On the day before the wedding Lucy got up early and went into the bathroom. She'd been to the chemist the day before and had bought the necessary package. She was ten days late! Ten whole days. Again she told herself it was probably a change in lifestyle, a change in diet, her constant worries about the future.

With trembling fingers she tore off the packaging before preparing her urine sample. Her fingers were dithering so much she could hardly hold the container still.

As the thin blue line appeared Lucy sat down on the loo, her legs trembling with shock.

Her first thought was to wonder how Vittorio would react when she told him he was going to be a father.

She would have to tell him. She owed him that. True, he loved children, family was important to him. But in effect she'd already left him.

And supposing there really was another woman…a mistress in Milan? How was he feeling about Lucy now she'd insisted on coming back to England? She wouldn't blame him if he'd already given up on her completely.

In the days they'd been apart, had he had time to review the situation? Had he decided that she wasn't the sort of woman he wanted to be with any more?

'I'm pregnant!' she told her reflection in the mirror.

In spite of the uncertainty of her situation she felt deliriously happy that she was going to become a mother. She needed some kind of celebration. A fanfare! Something to tell the world that she felt as if she was the only woman to be carrying a child.

Now that it had actually happened she couldn't think what she wanted to do about it. Since her miscarriage, she'd managed to convince herself it wouldn't happen, it would never happen!

But now…her whole world had changed.

She went back into her bedroom and dragged on an old pair of jeans that had somehow been pushed to the back of the wardrobe since her schooldays. Pulling a sweater over her head—early mornings in October were chilly in this part of the Yorkshire dales—she went down to the kitchen. The cat purred round her ankles, begging to be fed.

She looked in the fridge and chose a piece of fresh fish. Tinned cat food wasn't good enough for tortoise-shell Topsy today. Lucy was celebrating! Topsy looked down at her cat bowl, hardly able to believe her good fortune as she began to nibble at the fish.

'I'm going to have a baby, Topsy,' Lucy whispered

happily, but the cat seemed more interested in her breakfast.

That finished, Lucy went out into the garden, heading downwards towards the lane that led to the river. She'd no idea where she was going. She just knew she needed to escape. Maybe she could commune with a cow or a sheep? Maybe she was losing her mind? Perhaps she wasn't really pregnant. Maybe she'd read the test wrong...

All she knew was that she felt as if she was the happiest woman in the world. It didn't matter about the problems that would arise when she came to her senses and reviewed the practicalities. She wanted this baby. She'd wanted a baby ever since she'd lost the last one. And now it had actually happened. Perhaps it was compensation for losing the baby's father. But she wasn't going to dwell on that at the moment. She was simply going to assimilate the astounding idea that at long last she was going to be a mother.

She could see the mist rising over the water as she walked down the first part of the lane. The walls were too high to see the river now. She looked down at her scruffy walking boots, remembering how she'd walked down this lane so often on her way to school, checking to see that her shoes would pass inspection. One day the headmistress had sent her to one of the ancient outbuildings with a brush and some polish...

Oh, the shame! But she didn't care now. She didn't care about anything except the fact she was pregnant.

'I'm going to have a baby,' she told a startled sheep as it ran across the lane.

It bleated pitifully as if anxious to get away from this madwoman who was skipping down the lane on her thick-soled boots.

"'Season of mists and mellow fruitfulness…'" she began, putting as much expression as she could into the poem about autumn that her favourite teacher had taught her when she'd been a pupil at the village school.

Lucy thought carefully as the words of the poem escaped her. 'Start again. It was something about close-bosomed…'

'What's that about bosoms?'

She looked up at the man who was standing beside a blue car. For an instant, with the sun shining straight into her eyes, she thought she was hallucinating. It couldn't be!

'Vittorio! What are you…? Why are you here?'

'So I'm not welcome?'

'I didn't say that. I'm just stunned that's all. I thought you were in Rome. It is you, isn't it? I'm so surprised to see you here. Why are you parked here in the lane?'

'Because I can't find my way to the Montgomery residence. I flew into Manchester airport last night, stayed in a hotel, hired a car and got as far as the village. But there was nobody around to give me directions to your house. I was just about to go back to the village again when you came along, staring down at your feet, not looking where you were going and talking to yourself.'

'Oh, I'm so happy to see you. I've got some…' Suddenly she felt she couldn't disclose her momentous news here in the middle of the lane. 'How nice of you to come all this way,' she finished off in a stilted tone.

Vittorio gave an uneasy laugh. 'We're like a couple of strangers. Come here and let me hold you again.'

She hesitated as a nagging voice inside her head told her to stick to her resolution. But the sight of her handsome lover just standing there was simply too much for her.

'Oh, Vittorio, I've missed you,' she whispered as he drew her into the circle of his embrace.

'I've been missing you...too much,' he said quietly, as he held her closely. 'We need to talk.'

'Yes, yes we do. I've got...' No, she knew she couldn't tell him her news here in the middle of the lane. 'Let's go over that stile there. We can walk down by the river and talk without being disturbed.'

He held out his hand to help her over the stile. She was careful not to jump down the other side as she'd done so many times as a child.

She hugged the secret to herself, wondering how long it would be before she blurted out her amazing news. And wondering also what Vittorio's reaction would be.

He took her hand as they walked along the path down to the river. Lucy could feel the sun warm on her face now. She chose a favourite spot near the waterfall, out of the wind.

'We used to have picnics here when I was a child,' she said, picking up a flat stone and skimming it across the water that was still smooth as it moved ever closer towards the turbulence at the edge of the waterfall.

She sat down on a dry flat rock, facing the river. Vittorio crouched beside her, still holding her hand.

'Lucy, I've had a terrible time without you,' he began. 'After you left, it was just like my worst nightmare. Everything I'd vowed I wouldn't risk was happening again. The woman I loved had gone.'

'I didn't know you loved me...really loved me,' she said quietly.

'Of course I love you. I just didn't dare to admit it...not even to myself...until you left me. And then I realised how much I'd changed since you came into my life.'

'Vittorio I'm sorry that you suffered when your wife died but—'

'It wasn't just losing my wife and child!' Vittorio said heatedly. 'It was also the guilt I felt.'

She clutched his hand as he closed his eyes, seemingly reliving that dreadful day when his whole life had changed.

'I have always felt guilty that I didn't save my wife and son. They were both still alive when they were brought into Pronto Soccorso. I was in charge of the team that tried to save them and…and I failed them.'

'They were brought in when you were in charge of Pronto Soccorso?' she echoed in a strangled voice, unable to imagine the horror of such an occurrence. 'How were they injured?'

'My wife was driving the car. My little nine-month-old son, Ricardo, was strapped into his car seat. A lorry crossed the central reservation and crashed into them.' He paused and took a deep breath. 'My wife's car was crushed underneath it. The emergency services brought them into Pronto Soccorso. I didn't know who they were until I started to treat them…'

'Oh, Vittorio!' She knelt down in front of him, taking his face in her hands as she looked up into his anguished eyes. 'How did you…?

He took a deep breath. 'They were both still breathing. I did everything I could. The team were helping me…but it was too late. For over an hour we battled to save them. But first my little treasure died. And then my wife went… I've always thought there must have been something I could have done, something that—'

'No, Vittorio, you mustn't think like that! You are the most skilled doctor I've ever met in the whole of my career in Accident and Emergency.'

A sudden thought occurred to her. 'Was that why you changed to orthopaedics?'

He nodded. 'I knew I could never again go through the trauma of having to treat my own family in such a tragic situation. And that was why I've never wanted to risk such anguish again. Never wanted to risk taking on a wife and a child that might be taken from me. And when you left me to come to England, it was my worst nightmare really happening. Oh, we weren't married, we didn't have children, but you've become part of me. But I now realise that when you love somebody deeply, it's a risk you have to take.'

As she listened to Vittorio talking Lucy knew exactly what she had to do.

'I've come to the same conclusion,' she said quietly. 'Life is all about taking risks. We can't avoid commitment if we love somebody, even if we might find our hearts breaking when we lose them.'

Vittorio gave a sigh of relief. 'So you really understand now why I was so wary of commitment while we were together in Rome?'

'Yes, I understand.'

'But now...Lucy.' He cleared his throat. 'Now that we fully understand each other, Lucy, will you marry me?'

'I...' She stood up and took a few steps along the bank of the swirling river. Vittorio followed her, putting a hand lightly on her waist. She turned and looked up into his eyes.

'I've got something to tell you, Vittorio.'

'Please, you have to give me an answer first!'

'No, first I have to give you my news...our news.'

He put both hands on the sides of her shoulders. 'Our news? What do you mean?'

His eyes opened wider. The suspense was unbearable. 'You don't mean you're…?'

'I'm pregnant.'

'Oh, *caro mia, mio tresore*…what can I say?'

He held her against him as if he would never let her go.

'I gather that you're pleased, then?'

'Pleased? I'm over the moon. Do you realise that until a few weeks ago I was infertile? After the difficult birth of Ricardo I was asked to undergo a vasectomy. That's why I had to go to Milan…for a reversal of the operation.'

'So that's what you were doing in Milan? And all the time I thought… Oh, it doesn't matter now. I wasn't even sure I was still fertile after my miscarriage.'

One day she would tell him about how worried she'd been about her fertility. But today was a day for rejoicing, not dwelling on the past. It was the future that was all that mattered now.

'So, what's your answer, Lucy?'

'My answer to what?' she said innocently. 'Remind me, Vittorio.'

Vittorio smiled. As Lucy watched him go down on one knee on the wet morning grass beside the river, she noticed the deepening green stain seeping across his expensive trouser leg. But it didn't matter. Nothing mattered now, except that the two of them were back together again…for the rest of their lives.

He kissed her tenderly after she'd accepted his proposal, before lifting her in his arms and carrying her gently back to the car.

'Are you ready to meet my family?' she whispered as he set her down on her feet so that he could open the car door.

'I'm ready for anything now that you've made me the happiest man in the world.'

Vittorio swung open the car door and reached for her again. He was laughing with joy as he prepared to lift her off her feet and swing her round in the air.

'On second thoughts perhaps I shouldn't swing the mother of my child around,' he said, setting her feet down on the lane once more.

The farmer driving his cows down the lane was amazed to see a couple locked in a passionate embrace, seemingly totally oblivious to the outside world. Only when one of the cows nuzzled its wet nose against the woman did either of them show any reaction. The man, still with his arm around the woman, helped her into the car.

They were both smiling so happily the farmer decided they must have won the lottery.

'Nowt so queer as folks!' he muttered to himself as he walked beside his herd, guiding them with his stick so that they wouldn't scratch the stranger's fancy car.

It was only when he got down to the river that it occurred to him that the woman he'd seen might have been one of them Montgomery twins, grown-up, of course.

Yes, they'd been bonny girls and that skinny woman with the blonde hair must have been one of them. Now, was she the one that was getting married in the church tomorrow? He scratched his head. Like two peas in a pod they'd been when they'd swum down there in the river...

The organist was playing the Wedding March. Clinging tightly to Vittorio's hand, Lucy turned to watch her sister coming down the aisle.

'Oh, she looks so beautiful!'

'You'll look even more beautiful, Lucy,' Vittorio whispered. 'Can we book the church for next month?'

'How about Christmas?' Lucy whispered back. 'It's wonderful up here in the Dales at Christmas. Snow on the hills, carol services in the church, log fires in the house…'

'I think you've just talked me into it. Sounds wonderful! So long as you come down the aisle and tell me what to do when I'm standing up there like poor Carlos is doing at this moment.'

'Poor Carlos? He's loving every minute! And so will you, Vittorio. And so will you.'

And he did. As Vittorio stood in front of the altar a few weeks later, holly and ivy festooning the beautiful church, snow outside falling from the leaden skies, the promise of the warmth of a true Yorkshire Christmas on the following day, he felt that he'd never been so happy. And as his bride came down the aisle on her father's arm he thought she looked more beautiful than he'd ever seen her look.

As she drew close to him, lifting her beautiful white veil so that he could see her lovely face, he lowered his head as if to kiss her. Lucy's mouth was twitching and she was shaking her head almost imperceptibly.

'Not yet,' she whispered. 'Later…!'

And later, as they lay together in the bridal suite of the nearby hotel that Vittorio had reserved for their wedding night, he knew that the 'later' promised by his bride had been worth waiting for. Their marriage vows had already been consummated a couple of times, but he felt he couldn't get enough of this heavenly woman who was soon to be the mother of his child.

'I've booked the church for the christening to coincide with Sarah's and Carlos's first wedding anniversary,' Lucy said, as she snuggled closer.

Vittorio lay back against the pillows and smiled. 'Sounds like a real family reunion.'

Lucy smiled happily. 'Charlotte will be able to lord it over her baby cousin.'

'I love family reunions,' Vittorio said, as he reached out again towards Lucy. 'We were made to have a big family, don't you think?'

Lucy smiled as she felt her body responding to Vittorio's tantalising caresses.

'One baby at a time…?' she whispered as she gave herself up to the familiar feelings that Vittorio always inspired in her…

EPILOGUE

IN THE event, it turned out that having one baby at a time wasn't an option! When Lucy went for her three-month scan, she discovered she was carrying twins—both boys!

So when she and Vittorio finally arrived at the village church again, the following October, it was quite a performance. Carlos was godfather to Charles and an old friend of the Montgomery family was godfather to Henry.

'Well, twins are a tradition in our family,' Lucy had told everybody when she'd first discovered that she was carrying two babies.

'That's a good start to our family,' Vittorio whispered, as they watched their twin sons being lowered towards the font.

Both of them were protesting loudly as the vicar poured the holy water over their foreheads.

'Just like their father,' Lucy whispered. 'Hell bent on voicing their opinions.'

'If you want my opinion now, I'll give it to you,' Vittorio said. 'I think I'm the luckiest man in the world.'

Lucy smiled. 'I was just thinking I was the luckiest woman in the world.'

'Maybe we were made for each other,' Vittorio said, lowering his head so that he could kiss the mother of their first two babies.

'I don't care if that isn't an English tradition,' he

whispered as he raised his head. 'I just felt like saying thank you to the most beautiful woman in the world…'

Lucy could feel the familiar sensual excitement running through her. 'Maybe we could get together after the ceremony tonight? When our babies are asleep, of course.'

'Strangely enough, I was thinking exactly the same…'

Your opinion is important to us!

Please take a few moments to share your thoughts with us about Mills & Boon® and Silhouette® books. Your comments will ensure that we continue to deliver books you love to read.

To thank you for your input, everyone who replies will be entered into a prize draw to win a year's supply of their favourite series books*.

1. There are several different series under the Mills & Boon and Silhouette brands. Please tick the box that most accurately represents your reading habit for each series.

Series	Currently Read (have read within last three months)	Used to Read (but do not read currently)	Do Not Read
Mills & Boon			
Modern Romance™	❑	❑	❑
Sensual Romance™	❑	❑	❑
Blaze™	❑	❑	❑
Tender Romance™	❑	❑	❑
Medical Romance™	❑	❑	❑
Historical Romance™	❑	❑	❑
Silhouette			
Special Edition™	❑	❑	❑
Superromance™	❑	❑	❑
Desire™	❑	❑	❑
Sensation™	❑	❑	❑
Intrigue™	❑	❑	❑

2. Where did you buy this book?

From a supermarket ❑   Through our Reader Service™ ❑
From a bookshop ❑   If so please give us your Club Subscription no.
On the Internet ❑

_____ / _____

Other _____

3. Please indicate by number which were the 3 most important factors that made you buy this book. (1 = most important).

The picture on the cover ___   I enjoy this series ___
The author ___   The price ___
The title ___   I borrowed/was given this book ___
The description on the back cover ___   Part of a mini-series ___

Other _____

4. How many Mills & Boon and /or Silhouette books do you buy at one time?

I buy ___ books at one time ❑
I rarely buy a book (less than once a year) ❑

5. How often do you shop for any Mills & Boon and/or Silhouette books?

One or more times a month ❑   A few times per year ❑
Once every 2-3 months ❑   Never ❑

6. How long have you been reading Mills & Boon® and/or Silhouette®?
_____ years

7. What other types of book do you enjoy reading?

Family sagas eg. Maeve Binchy ❏
Classics eg. Jane Austen ❏
Historical sagas eg. Josephine Cox ❏
Crime/Thrillers eg. John Grisham ❏
Romance eg. Danielle Steel ❏
Science Fiction/Fantasy eg. JRR Tolkien ❏
Contemporary Women's fiction eg. Marian Keyes ❏

8. Do you agree with the following statements about Mills & Boon? Please tick the appropriate boxes.

	Strongly agree	Tend to agree	Neither agree nor disagree	Tend to disagree	Strongly disagree
Mills & Boon offers great value for money.	❏	❏	❏	❏	❏
With Mills & Boon I can always find the right type of story to suit my mood.	❏	❏	❏	❏	❏
I read Mills & Boon books because they offer me an entertaining escape from everyday life.	❏	❏	❏	❏	❏
Mills & Boon stories have improved or stayed the same standard over the time I have been reading them.	❏	❏	❏	❏	❏

9. Which age bracket do you belong to? Your answers will remain confidential.

❏ 16-24   ❏ 25-34   ❏ 35-49   ❏ 50-64   ❏ 65+

THANK YOU for taking the time to tell us what you think! If you would like to be entered into the **FREE prize draw** to win a year's supply of your favourite series books, please enter your name and address below.

Name: _____

Address: _____

_____

Post Code: _____   Tel: _____

Please send your completed questionnaire to the address below:

READER SURVEY, PO Box 676, Richmond, Surrey, TW9 1WU.

LRI 958   GL 886

FREE!

4 Books
and a surprise gift!

We would like to take this opportunity to thank you for reading this Mills & Boon® book by offering you the chance to take FOUR more specially selected titles from the Medical Romance™ series absolutely FREE! We're also making this offer to introduce you to the benefits of the Reader Service™—

- ★ **FREE home delivery**
- ★ **FREE gifts and competitions**
- ★ **FREE monthly Newsletter**
- ★ **Exclusive Reader Service offers**
- ★ **Books available before they're in the shops**

Accepting these FREE books and gift places you under no obligation to buy, you may cancel at any time, even after receiving your free shipment. Simply complete your details below and return the entire page to the address below. You don't even need a stamp!

YES! Please send me 4 free Medical Romance books and a surprise gift. I understand that unless you hear from me, I will receive 6 superb new titles every month for just £2.69 each, postage and packing free. I am under no obligation to purchase any books and may cancel my subscription at any time. The free books and gift will be mine to keep in any case.

M4ZEF

Ms/Mrs/Miss/Mr ....Initials.....................................
                                                                                    BLOCK CAPITALS PLEASE
Surname ....
Address..

....

....Postcode...................................

Send this whole page to to:
UK: FREEPOST CN81, Croydon, CR9 3WZ